Circle of Joy

AVALON NURSE & CAREER SERIES

CIRCLE OF JOY

Dorothy Collett

AVALON BOOKS
THOMAS BOUREGY AND COMPANY, INC.
NEW YORK

PRINTED IN THE UNITED STATES OF AMERICA
BY HADDON CRAFTSMEN, SCRANTON, PENNSYLVANIA

Circle of Joy

CHAPTER ONE

"The owner's name is Cole Bradshaw," the woman from the employment agency said. "Chicken International is the name of the restaurant. Got that, hon?"

Hunching the phone into her shoulder while she made notes, Pam asked, "Why would they want a layout artist in a restaurant? What exactly is this job, anyway?"

"Design coordinator, whatever that is," Mrs. Perlman said, naming a salary that made Pam gasp. "We got the order ten minutes ago and are giving you first crack at it. He really didn't explain things too clearly. But he wants a recent art student. Any kind of art. Advertising or architecture or fine arts or interior decorating. Anything like that. He wants to interview you at one this afternoon, and he'll be able to tell you all about the job then. Now write down the directions to the restaurant."

Pam scribbled on distractedly. It was already eleven. Her two best job-hunting outfits were at the cleaner's. Furthermore, she didn't have the foggiest notion what a design coordinator was, what she should add or remove from her portfolio when applying for the job. Why, oh, why hadn't the man explained things more clearly to the people at the employment agency? It was kind of nice to know just what kind of work one was applying for.

"Better luck this time, dear," the woman was saying. "And let us know how you make out."

Pam hung up and flew around her tiny apartment, pulling herself together for the job interview.

At ten to one she was driving slowly and carefully along the narrow causeway that led to the small offshore California island. Thank goodness, she thought for the thousandth time in the last two days, it was her left wrist that was incapacitated in its rigid cast, making one-handed driving possible.

The soothing combination of the warm summer breeze and the sound and smell of the gently rippling Pacific dissipated some of her pre-interview nervousness.

She was on the island now, heading for the low, sprawling building nestling behind a jungle of bougainvillea and creeping juniper. As she drew closer, she saw the tastefully lettered CHICKEN INTER-NATIONAL emblazoned on the canopy.

She circled the big parking lot, empty now except for a blue Datsun and a small, sedate-looking black Mercedes. She pulled into the slot beside the black sedan. That car would belong to this Cole Bradshaw, she thought.

Pam cut her motor and took a deep breath as she reached for her portfolio. The jerky movement caused her to wince in pain. Pressing two slender fingers to the purplish swelling on her forehead, she closed her amber eyes and blinked back the threatening tears. When the throbbing subsided, she fluffed out her auburn bangs to make sure they covered the disfiguring lump.

Getting out of the car, she smoothed her dark-blue skirt and, her portfolio tucked under the right arm, her canvas tote flung over her left shoulder, she firmed her tiny chin. Then she walked to the restaurant entrance.

Her rap on the locked door brought a short, stocky man in a big white apron to the doorway. "We don't open the restaurant till five, ma'am."

"I'm Pamela Harper," she said. "I was sent here by the Perlman Placement Service. I have an appointment with Mr. Bradshaw."

The man's florid face split into an apologetic grin. "I forgot." He stepped aside, and Pam walked into the sumptuous lobby. "I'll tell the boss you're here, Miss Harper."

He lumbered into the rear of the building, and Pam waited at the reservation desk, gazing at the dining room in admiration.

The enormous space was divided into a number of sections by a network of planters that were spilling over with vibrant greenery. The alcove to her right with the long, mirrored bar, the small tables, the huge piano was obviously the cocktail lounge.

To her left, in the main dining area, the chairs were all upside down on the tables. The only wall that didn't boast an ocean view was entirely covered with a colorful mural of the world, flanked by two magnificent roosters.

Pam had never been in a restaurant like this. It wasn't the kind of eatery Alan Wilson could afford on his schoolteacher's salary.

The man appeared so silently on the thick carpeting Pam didn't see him until he was towering over her, inches away.

He held out his hand. "Cole Bradshaw." His voice was deep, pleasant. "You must be Pamela Harper."

She took his hand and felt a prickling up her arm. "Yes, I'm here about the job," she said, her trained eye appraising him in that uncomfortable second. She saw a head of thick blond hair with a boyishly rebellious cowlick, blue eyes, and a strong, aristocratic nose. Prominent cheekbones tapered into a wide, firm mouth. He wasn't just attractive. He had the kind of rugged good looks that doubtlessly appealed to swarms of women.

"We'll talk in my office." With an easy smile, he cupped her right elbow and led her into the back, through a huge kitchen full of impressive chrome applicances, some of which Pam couldn't identify.

"That's Art, our head chef, getting started with tonight's fare," he said, nodding toward the man who'd let her in and was now bent over one of the big work tables, busily examining some vegetables to make sure they were flawless.

Releasing her elbow, Cole Bradshaw opened another door.

Pam followed him down a long corridor, her gaze sweeping across the brown jacket straining over his powerful shoulders.

Inside his plush office, he indicated a chair for her, then sat down behind his massive desk.

"Now," he said, "Mrs. Perlman did explain what we're looking for, didn't she?"

Pam tried to think of a tactful answer. "She said you were looking for a design coordinator, but she didn't go into any detail."

"Well, the job will involve several different things, including some advertising illustration. The Enright Agency has been doing all our ad work until now. But I'd prefer us to do our own stuff."

She wondered if the Enright Agency, San Diego's top ad shop, had displeased him. If so, in what way? But, afraid of antagonizing the man, she didn't ask.

His eyes focused on her arm cast, he quickly changed the subject. "Mrs. Perlman said you'd had some sort of accident, but she didn't go into details about that either."

"It happened downtown Wednesday morning," Pam said. "I'd just left Farnsworth's Department Store. When I started across the street, a driver ran the stoplight and would have hit me if a pedestrian hadn't pushed me out of the car's path."

It had all been written up in yesterday

morning's paper, but Cole Bradshaw wouldn't have seen it, buried way in the back as it was.

"So I was lucky." Pam forced a bright smile she hoped hid the anger and self-pity she couldn't shake off. "I ended up with this small fracture in my wrist." She held up her left arm. Then, with her right hand, she began digging into her portfolio. "You'll want to see some of my work and my resume." She found the neatly typed paper and held it out to him.

But he didn't take it. He was frowning at her. "What were you doing at Farnsworth's?"

She laid the resume on his desk. "Applying for a job in their advertising department."

He softly said, "And they didn't hire you?"

Detecting a note of sympathy in his voice, Pam stiffened her spine. "They did hire me, but they were in a bind and needed somebody to start right away. And since I'm supposed to take it easy next week on account of the..." She caught herself in time. She'd almost said "concussion." But since he couldn't possibly have seen the newspaper story, he didn't know about that. And there wasn't any point in giving him the chance to wonder if there might be something wrong with her head.

"So they couldn't hold it for me," she finished lamely. "Mrs. Perlman said you didn't need anybody for another week, so she sent me here."

"That's right. But I'd like to know why they didn't get this guy who cost you that other job and..." He glanced down at the cast. "And that."

"The driver just kept going. Nobody got the license number. The witnesses couldn't even agree on the description of the car." She paused to get rid of the bitterness that had crept into her voice. "They did say the car lurched all over the street as it sped away. The police said the driver was probably drunk."

Cole Bradshaw's eyes clouded, and he sighed heavily as he picked up the typed sheet that told him she had graduated with honors from Amberson College where she'd majored in fine arts and minored in advertising. Her only working experience consisted of being a "part-time waitress at Pete's Pizza Palace."

"I see you have some restaurant experience," he said.

"I waitressed at Pete's while I was going to college," she said. "Until three months ago when they went bankrupt."

He didn't comment about that. Instead he asked, "You live with your family?"

"I live in my own apartment," she said. "When my dad retired two years ago, he sold our house and bought a camper. Now he and Mom are roaming around the country." She didn't quite know what to say next. "I didn't see any need to add that to my resume," she finished stiffly.

"And you were right." Mr. Bradshaw's smile was reassuring. "Your personal life has nothing to do with the job. I had no business asking."

She reached into her portfolio and sorted through the fat sheaf of drawings from school. "Speaking of the job," she went on pleasantly, handing them to him, "I brought some of my artwork." She dug deeper. "And these are volunteer projects I'm currently working on for Pet Haven." She gave him a colorful poster of a woebegone puppy and a scruffy kitten gazing wistfully at each other. Below the picture were the words: BARGAINS FOR YOU, SURVIVAL FOR US.

"This one," she explained, "is to be displayed in the window of our new thrift shop." While he studied it, she pulled out a watercolor placard of a shelf of books. "And this one is for the used-book section."

He took that, finally exclaiming with a surprised kind of admiration, "When Mrs. Perlman said you were good, she was putting it mildly."

Pam covered her pleasure with an offhand, "I haven't done the lettering on it yet, but it will say: NEXT TO PETS, BOOKS ARE MAN'S BEST FRIENDS."

He handed them back to her with a warm grin. "If I had had any doubts about your ability to fill our needs, they're dead and buried."

"What *are* your needs?" she asked, his extravagant approval bolstering her self-confidence.

"Ads for the newspapers, TV, magazines, Chamber of Commerce brochures." He leaned forward, his arms folded across his desk as a new excitement came into his voice. "We're going to need to redesign our dinner menus, and we want to change our cocktail napkins, with the same design carried out in matchbook covers. We want to keep the place looking attractive. We have to rearrange the plant decor from time to time." His smile stretched into a wide grin. "With the mortality rate so high among restaurants, we have to keep offering something new. Different lights, a new floor covering. Change the cocktail lounge maybe, and so forth."

"I could do it," she said eagerly, while wondering if these things could actually add up to a full-time permanent job.

He riffled through his own papers, finally looking up at her again. "Will you be able to start next Friday, Pam, a week from today?"

She let out her breath. She had the job! Just like that! "Friday will be perfect." She struggled to keep her relief hidden under a businesslike tone. She even managed to keep a professional cool when he confirmed the fabulous salary figure previously mentioned by Mrs. Perlman.

He smiled. "As you probably know, we have another Chicken International in Los Angeles. I spend the early part of the week up there, weekends here, returning by airplane. And I usually manage to spend Mondays with my mother. That's when we're closed here. So when I'm not here, you'll be working with Jerry Crandell, our manager at this branch. But I'll be back next Friday when you start." He rolled his chair away from his desk and edged forward in his seat. He was finished. He'd hired her.

But Pam wasn't quite finished. "What will my hours be, Mr. Bradshaw?"

"The hours are loose. After all, this isn't a time-clock kind of a job." He made an impatient gesture with his hands. "You'll probably want to take some work home with you at times. You'll be spending a lot of time at a television studio, supervising the commercial you've created. You'll have to shop for whatever supplies you'll need." His sudden half smile was almost apologetic. "I guess it's a case of checking into your office every day, taking off when you need to, closing up for the day here no later than six o'clock."

"The Pet Haven meetings are on Sundays," she said tentatively, her original elation clouded by her Sunday commitment. "And Sundays must be one of the biggest days here. But, of course, a job like this is more important, so if you need me then—"

"What is this Pet Haven?" he cut in curiously.

"It's a shelter for stray, injured, or abandoned cats and dogs," she answered. "But, as I say, I can drop out."

"No problem," he said easily. "There's no need for you to check in here on Sundays. And, as I told you, we're all off on Mondays." His smile stretched indulgently. "It'll be like your volunteer job, Pam. Jerry or I will tell you what's needed, and you'll take it from there. Or maybe you'll see a need and go ahead on your own. It's up to you to set your hours to suit yourself. No problem. All you have to do is make sure everything about this place looks right—the lights, the furniture, the ads, the bathroom sinks, everything. Okay?"

"Fine," she said crisply, chiding herself for acting so naive. She'd just been offered a staff position in the Big Time where you were hired for performance, not attendance, and she'd reacted like a frightened file clerk. "And thank you, Mr. Bradshaw. You won't be sorry." She stood and reached for her samples, stuffing them back into her portfolio.

He was up too, coming around the desk. "I know I won't." He walked her to the front door. At the entrance he added, "And one more thing, Pam. We don't stand on ceremony here. It's strictly first names among the staff. We're a team working together, friends. It makes for a good working atmosphere. So no more Mr. Bradshaw."

"Cole then," she murmured. With a parting smile, she started briskly toward her car.

Somehow she sensed he was watching her, but she didn't turn until she was behind the steering wheel, the motor on.

He was still standing there. She waved. He gave a small salute and walked inside.

CHAPTER TWO

As Pam headed east toward Woodland, her heart sang with joy. She had a job. A wonderful job. It was like a miracle. It *was* a miracle. In her wildest fantasies she couldn't have conjured up anything this perfect. Her duties sounded like sheer fun. The place was heavenly. The boss couldn't have been nicer. And the salary! She had to pinch herself to make sure she wasn't dreaming.

She was still marveling at her good fortune when she reached the older part of the community and pulled into the driveway alongside a small stucco duplex that had seen better days. When she saw her landlord clipping the hedge that separated his property from the real estate office next door, she was guiltily glad he hadn't seen her drive in.

Much as she usually enjoyed talking to Mr. Hanson, she was too excited today to engage in a long conversation with him. She picked up her mail without glancing at it and flew up the stairs to her studio apartment.

Inside, she kicked off her shoes, dropped her portfolio and tote bag, put the mail down on the counter, and hoisted herself up on a high stool. Reaching for the wall phone, she dialed the employment agency to report her good news to Mrs. Perlman. When she hung up, after being thoroughly congratulated, she picked up the mail.

Tossing the bills aside, she glanced at the picture postcard from Alan Wilson — a colorful photograph of one of San Francisco's famed cable cars.

It's good to see Mom and Dad again, but I'll be glad to get back to San Diego Saturday next, he'd written. *Too many memories here.*

Poor Alan, she thought, still carrying a torch for that girl who'd walked out on him three years ago, a girl who'd wanted a singing career more than she'd wanted Alan. He'd had to get away from San Francisco after that. Now he was teaching at Woodland High, with his summer job at the community center playground beginning a week from Monday.

Pam remembered how much she'd liked him when they met at one of the Pet Haven meetings shortly after he'd moved to San Diego, how quickly they'd become fast friends. It had been an ideal arrangement for both of them, with Alan unable to forget the girl he couldn't have and with Pam too involved with school and her part-time job at Pete's Pizza Palace for any romantic entanglements.

It had been Alan who'd told her about this apartment in the building where he lived. "It's small," he'd warned then, two years ago. "It's really just an add-on, but it's cheap."

She'd loved everything about it: the cozy privacy, the nice floor, the big old eucalyptus trees outside the windows. From where she sat now at the counter in the tiny kitchenette, she could see her big drawing board, her sofa bed, and her easy chair. If she craned her neck, she could see the built-in closets that lined the hall, which led to the compact bathroom.

It *was* small, but she still loved it.

The next morning Pam was perched on a stool at the counter sipping her third cup of coffee when the phone rang.

"We were so busy at the shop all day yesterday, I didn't get a chance to phone you." It was Kate Daye, her voice muffled over all the chattering in the background. "We're still rushed here, unpacking a huge shipment of French dolls and some very fragile antique Swedish dolls, but I had to make sure you're getting along okay and to tell you I'll be glad to pick you up at one tomorrow if you're up to going to the Pet Haven meeting."

Usually Pam rode with Alan. But since he'd been gone, she and Kate had been taking turns driving. And this week it was her turn. Still, it was a long trip.

"I'm up to the meeting," Pam told Kate, "but maybe not the driving. So I'll sure appreciate the lift. I'm more than okay, though," she added, anxious to share her good news. "In fact, I'm wonderful. I got another job. I was just going to call you."

"Congratulations," Kate squealed. "You don't waste time. What? Where? How? When?"

With a fresh surge of excitement, Pam answered the barrage of questions. "Design coordinator at Chicken International. Through the Perlman Agency. I start next Friday." Then she named the salary she still couldn't believe. "And the owner of the restaurant couldn't be nicer."

"Sounds like losing that Farnsworth's job was a blessing in disguise," Kate exclaimed. "Tell me all about him."

"I'll give you a detailed report on the ride out tomorrow," Pam promised.

When they hung up, Pam moved over to her drawing board to finish the lettering on the book placard. While she worked, she let her thoughts drift back to the past.

She couldn't remember a time when she hadn't felt a compulsion to draw or paint. An only child, Pam had come as an astonishing surprise to her middle-aged parents. Devoted to each other, with old-fashioned values, they'd loved their independent daughter but hadn't understood her absorption in art, her determination to have a successful career as some kind of commercial artist. They couldn't understand her lack of interest in the carefree fun they considered normal for a pretty young girl.

"Is it right to use a fine charity like that for your own gain?" Mom had asked when she'd become involved with Pet Haven...because she'd wanted to do posters and other artwork for them, artwork she could include in her portfolio— to show prospective employers!

"But it isn't as if I won't still be helping the poor little animals," Pam had argued.

So she'd gone ahead, and her membership in the Pet Haven organization had

led to her close friendship with some of
the other volunteers, particularly with
Alan, who was in charge of the shelter's
quarterly newsletter, which she illus-
trated. And with Kate, who supervised
the various fund-raising events because
she owned and operated a successful doll
shop.

"We wouldn't have taken in nearly this
much money," Kate had gloated after
their last white-elephant bazaar, "if it
hadn't been for your marvelous posters,
Pam."

Pam had glowed with pleasure as she'd
carefully wrapped them up to take home,
so they could be added to her portfolio.

By the time her father had retired
from his job at the start of her third year
in college, she was an integral part of the
Pet Haven foundation. She'd known her
parents' concern for her was delaying
their long-held dream of spending their
well-earned leisure years on the road, so,
with Alan's help, she'd taken off on her
own.

A month later, when her father sold
the house, bought the camper, and arranged for a modest monthly payment to

see her through to graduation, Pam's life was full and busy.

She sighed now, as she inked in the last letter on her book poster. The next time her parents phoned from wherever they were, and she told them about her fabulous new job at the restaurant, they were bound to feel proud of her.

It was three when Pam's phone rang again. "Cole Bradshaw here," the deep voice said. "Pam?"

Her heart skipped a beat. Was he withdrawing his offer? "Yes," she said weakly.

"It occurred to me you should see our restaurant in action, see it from the vantage point of the customer, sample our food, meet our crew. So if by some miracle you're free tonight, how about letting me show you the working side of our operation?"

He wasn't withdrawing the job offer. Relieved and excited, she said gaily, "As it happens, my boyfriend is out of town, so I am free."

"Good. I'll pick you up at six."

The line went dead. It was a minute before Pam realized he hadn't asked for her address. And he hadn't written down her phone number during the interview. Of course the address and phone number had been on her resume. Could he have remembered them? Maybe he'd gotten them from Mrs. Perlman or looked her up in the phone book—or something. That must be it.

It was another minute before her face-saving words played back—*my boy-friend*. Well, Alan was a boy—if you could call a twenty-nine-year-old man a boy. And he certainly was a friend. And they would probably be doing something together tonight if he was in town. Also, much to her dismay, lately Pam had been feeling a warmth for Alan that went beyond friendship, a feeling that was futile.

Pushing Alan out of her mind, Pam started to get ready a little after five. Slipping the waterproofed enclosure over her cast, she managed the shower and a one-handed shampoo. While she brushed her auburn hair shiny dry, she was glad it was short and curly enough to arrange without the bother of a dryer.

Rummaging through her closet, she pulled out her apricot sundress with its flattering neckline and billowing skirt. If it was a little on the dressy side for a business meeting, this was kind of a date too, wasn't it?

It was, after all, Saturday night. But a date? Another little worry nibbled at her. What if her new boss was married? If he was, then would his wife be there too? For some reason, that possibility was most unappealing.

CHAPTER THREE

A few minutes after six the ring of the bell sent Pam flying to the door.

Cole, resplendent in trim white cords and a navy blazer, greeted her with a jovial, "All set for a sneak preview of your new job?"

"Looking forward to it," she murmured, covering her sudden shyness with a warm smile. Why had it seemed so different when she was talking to this man in his office?

As they stepped outside, he moved around to avoid touching her left arm. Instead he took her right elbow in his hand as he guided her down the steps.

The sight of the small black Mercedes parked in the driveway didn't surprise her.

"It's a lovely car," she said as he helped her into the passenger side, "but somehow..." She broke off, not knowing how to finish without voicing her impulsive thought—that such a conservative black automobile didn't seem to fit the man.

He chuckled as he strode around and settled himself at the wheel. "Not flashy enough for a guy like me?" he said lightly.

She averted her head so he wouldn't notice her flush.

The motor purred into life at his touch. The turn of a knob filled the car with faint strains of music. Accustomed to the labored motor of her elderly Honda, Pam was acutely aware of the leashed-in power of this staid little sedan.

Cole didn't speak again until they were in the traffic, heading toward the beach. "Actually, this is my mother's car. I use it when I'm in town." He glanced at Pam with a rueful smile. "But you're right. I'll admit I prefer my Jaguar.

That's the one I use when I'm in Los Angeles."

"You live with your mother when you're here?"

He nodded soberly. "I never moved out, and now that there are just the two of us..." His voice trailed off and, sensing his sudden withdrawal, Pam peeked at his profile. Just the two of them? Then that must mean he wasn't married.

They rode in silence, the outline of Cole's face set into thoughtful grooves. Rejecting the impulse to speculate on his preoccupation, Pam concentrated instead on the silky rhythm of the car.

Her breath caught when they reached the end of the long causeway. The little island had become alive. The lowering sun was casting a magical glow over the whole place. Now the parking lot was full of expensive cars, and well-dressed couples milled around. As Cole pulled up to the canopied entrance, the floodlights came on.

"Evening, Mr. Bradshaw," the uniformed doorman greeted Cole as he opened Pam's door.

Pam didn't hear Cole's response. The

wide restaurant door had opened, and her senses reeled from the savory aromas, the clinking of crystal and muted voices mingling with a slow, haunting tune from the piano.

In the lobby where Pam had waited yesterday to be interviewed by a prospective employer, the tuxedoed maitre d' was now giving her a deferential smile.

"Your table will be ready whenever you are," he told Cole.

"We're not in a hurry, Dick," Cole said, leading Pam into the more dimly lit lounge where he seated her at a choice corner table that seemed to be suspended over the ocean.

"It's beautiful," she exclaimed.

"I'm glad you like it here, Pam," Cole said softly. "It's important to me that all my employees find their surroundings pleasant."

Before Pam could tell him she was sure they all must, a miniskirted waitress appeared.

"My usual Scotch," he told her, with a questioning glance at Pam.

"Something fruity," she said helplessly, decrying the fact that her financial limitations hadn't allowed for familiarity with the cocktail world.

He gave her an amused look. Then he smiled and turned to the pretty waitress. "This is Barby, Pam. Ask Harv to concoct something fruity for Miss Harper."

Pam didn't care what they concocted for her. The heady experience of being wined and dined by the boss on his own glamorous turf wiped out her moment of embarrassment.

Until she felt his fingers trailing across hers. "No sensation here yet?" he asked anxiously.

"A tingling," she admitted. But only when he touched her. She had to force herself to pull her left arm away. She had to remind herself his touch was only a sympathetic gesture of concern.

Hiding her naive reaction, she asked lightly, "Tell me, do all your new employees get this red-carpet treatment?"

His eyebrows rose. "The important ones do." The smile came slowly. "I want my staff to feel comfortable here, Pam. As I told you yesterday, I find it makes for a better working atmosphere if we're all friends."

"Does that mean the new employees can interview the boss?" she asked boldly.

"By all means." He actually looked pleased. "Let's see—my resume goes like this. Thirty-two. Single. That covers the past and present." His lips twitched mischievously. "As for my future status, I'll confess to no prospects." He shrugged. "All in all, I'm not a bad guy. Do unto others and all that. Do I pass so far?"

With flying colors. But Pam didn't say that. Their drinks came, and, after another friendly exchange with the cute waitress, Cole lifted his glass and clinked it against Pam's. "To a long and mutually successful business association."

Not sure how to respond to the formal toast, Pam tasted a mouth-watering, mildly alcoholic mixture of coconut and pineapple. "Mmmm. It's delicious."

"Now how about the rest of my interview?" he prompted.

Encouraged, Pam moved on to her next question. "I can't help wondering how you manage two restaurants so far apart."

"I have excellent managers. I'm just a kind of troubleshooter and final-decision-maker. I'm back and forth, part of the week here, part there." He mentioned a small condo in Los Angeles and, again, his real home here in his mother's house.

Her curiosity goaded her on. "How did you happen to get started with all this?"

"I guess you could say it was by the accident of birth," Cole answered slowly, suddenly sobering. "My grandfather had a fish-and-chips shack on the beach. My dad was bored with the business. And when he got out of college, he spent two years bumming around the world. But the food business must have been in his blood. When Grandfather died, Dad came back with a collection of recipes, all the different ways various countries prepare chicken. He sold that place, figuratively mortgaged his soul to buy this little man-made island, and plunged headlong into this innovative concept. To make a long story as short as possible, my future here was inescapable."

"But there are two restaurants now."

"Yeah." Cole sighed, his eyes clouding

up, his voice thickening. "After I got the hang of things here, Dad left me in charge while he opened the second one in Los Angeles. Norman, my younger brother, was one year away from graduation then, and Dad's idea was to eventually leave one restaurant to each of us. So when the new place was off and running, I was sent up there to manage it, and Norm was trained to take over the San Diego branch. Dad did a lot of commuting back and forth. Everything was going according to plan until..."

When his voice choked away, he gulped down the last of his drink and turned to signal for another. "You ready, Pam?" Seeing her half-full glass, he asked, "Or do you want to try something different?"

With a shake of her head, she said, "This will take care of my liquid intake for the day."

When his second drink came, she waited until he'd sipped it before she said softly, "Everything went according to plan until when?"

"Until six months ago." A strange expression came into his eyes.

An icy sixth sense warned Pam not to ask any more questions.

But the tragic facts spewed out of him in spurts: The flimsy skiff overturning in a sudden squall. The bodies—Norman's and his father's—recovered too late.

Cole's raspy voice had gotten so low, Pam had to strain to hear the words. "I was out of town. Norm's wedding was a week away. Natalie—his fiancee—still hasn't accepted her loss. The poor, tormented girl." The tortured voice stopped.

While Pam searched for the right, comforting words, his hand came out over hers in a silent plea to drop the painful subject.

"Hungry?" he asked.

"Starved," she said.

When they sauntered into the elegant dining room, Pam was seated next to Cole in the only booth and handed a menu by one of the red-vested waiters.

"This is Sam," Cole said, introducing the smiling older man. "Sam has been with us from the beginning."

"Because it's the best place to be," Sam told Pam. Turning to Cole, he asked if they were ready to order.

Cole shook his head. "We'll just browse through the possibilities here."

Pam picked up the parchment menu, the pages bound with gold silk cording, her eyes widening as she scanned the fascinating entrees. There were ten mouth-watering chicken dishes to choose from. A brief description was given of each dish, and there was an amusing comment about the country or area where it had originated.

Noticing the absence of prices, Pam realized that the people who dined here wouldn't care.

When she looked up, Cole was watching her.

She said, "I'm going to have the chicken with peanuts and pineapple. How does that sound?"

He laughed. "If you don't object to the naughty romantic legend connected to it."

"I don't care what they say about it. It sounds wonderful." She was ravenous. "And I think your menus are a work of art. I can't imagine why you'd even consider wanting new ones."

"We're changing some of the entrees," he said.

As if by remote control, Sam was there, taking their orders and the menus.

When he left, Cole went on. "Our offering from Pakistan hasn't been going over too well, and we're not absorbing the soaring cost of the ingredients for the honey-spiced number from the Mediterranean countries. So we're considering substituting a tarragon concoction from France. And there are a couple of possibilities from Mexico in my dad's recipe collection. Also, we'll want a different look to the menu. Something fresh."

Pam said, "How about some drawings? It might be fun to have little sketches alongside the description of the dish. You know, like a native girl in a sarong balancing a basket of fruit on her head. Or a little fellow with a guitar and a sombrero. It's just a suggestion," she added nervously.

"But it's a nice idea." There was no mistaking the enthusiasm in his voice. "We *do* need you, Pam."

She lowered her eyes, embarrassed by his praise.

It was like a reprieve when a waiter sidled up to Cole to tell him he was wanted on the phone.

CHAPTER FOUR

After Cole had excused himself and
left the booth, Pam took a deep breath
and reinforced her cool. She felt increas-
ingly anxious to do a good job for him—
not only because this was such a
fabulous opportunity, but because she
wanted to justify his faith in her. She
surely would fit in, she told herself. She
loved this place. And certainly she had
the training and the talent to make a
success of the job.

By the time Cole returned, Pam's self-
confidence was back in full force. "I'm

ready to tie into that pineapple chicken," she reminded him gaily.

His eyes slid past her. "Good. Because I see it coming right up."

Pam was so hungry and the food was so luscious, she ate every last bite. When the pastry cart was wheeled over, Cole chose two nut-encrusted delicacies for them.

"Baklava," he said. "Compliments of Greece."

Pam couldn't hide her delight. "This place is like something out of the Arabian Nights. All that wonderful food. Eating here isn't just a dinner. It's an event."

Cole's pleasure wreathed his face. "Before we leave, I want you to meet Jerry. He'll have grabbed an early bite in his office. We both do it that way so we're free to come out here and mingle with the customers. Unless we're dining with a friend."

It wasn't the words that made Pam shiver. It was the warmth in his smile, the husky tone in his voice, the caressing melting softness in his blue eyes as they held hers.

It took all her will power to maintain a semblance of poise. "I'm glad I'm a friend."

His hand came out to touch hers so briefly she scarcely felt it. "I'm glad you're glad."

After they finished their demitasses, and Pam repaired her makeup in the luxuriously appointed powder room, Cole took her back into the EMPLOYEES ONLY area.

The whole atmosphere in the big kitchen had undergone a complete change. Now it was buzzing with activity as the three puffy-hatted chefs and their helpers worked with well-coordinated precision. Orders were given as tray-laden waiters moved in and out. The continual sounds of food preparation were joined by the festive noise from the dining room as the door to the kitchen kept opening.

Art, the head chef, glanced up long enough to give Pam a friendly little wave.

In the rear corridor, suddenly quiet as the inner door closed behind them, Pam was led into the office just past Cole's.

"This is Jerry Crandell, our manager, Pam," Cole introduced the man who was rising from his desk and coming toward them with a polite smile. "Pamela Harper, our new design coordinator," Cole told the nice-looking, neatly dressed man who wasn't quite as young or as tall or as attractive as he.

Pam held out her hand and murmured her acknowledgement.

"Welcome aboard, Miss Harper." The manager's smile and words were courteous. But there was a chilly glint in his gray eyes that made her stiffen. "It will be a pleasure working with you."

She forced a smile, a cordial tone. "I'll be grateful for your expert direction, Mr. Crandell."

The three of them chatted a few moments, but Pam had no idea what any of them said. She was too busy wondering why this man disliked her.

When they left, Cole said, "Jerry's a good guy. You'll like working with him."

"I'm sure I will," she managed, knowing Cole hadn't noticed the coldness underneath the man's polite words.

She was still puzzling over Jerry's hostile reaction to her when Cole maneuvered the Mercedes out of the parking lot and headed toward Woodland.

"You're a very sweet girl, Pam." His arm came casually around her shoulder. "You have talent and beauty. We're lucky to have you. Is it possible you're perfect?"

She giggled, relaxing into the companionable curve of his arm. "Not at all. I have lots of faults."

"Such as?" He sounded skeptical.

"For one thing," she said, suddenly serious, "perfect people are supposed to be forgiving, and I can't forgive that coward who ran the light. Whoever it was..." Her words trailed away in sudden confusion.

After all, in a crazy, roundabout way, she owed this job to that lawbreaker, didn't she?

"And," she rushed along, thinking of her stubborn determination to make her career in art, "they're not supposed to do whatever is expedient to get what they want the way I do."

"You wouldn't be human if you didn't

hate the guy who did this to you," Cole said. "And we all want what we want. If we want to be successful, we have to do whatever's necessary to reach our goal."

"It sounds as if you're saying you believe the end justifies the means."

He hesitated. "If it's a *good* end," he said. "If the means don't hurt anyone."

Her smile was radiant. "Thanks for letting me off the hook."

He laughed and pulled to a stop in front of her building. Gently disengaging his arm, he got out of the car and came around to her side. "And now you have almost a whole week to loaf."

"I wish I didn't need it," she admitted ruefully. "I'm really looking forward to getting started. I know I'm going to love it."

"If you're going to say that a week from tonight," he said, "you'll have to be in tip-top condition. So better do a lot of loafing while you can."

As he escorted her up the stairs, she fumbled in her purse for her key. It was dark. She'd forgotten to leave her outside light on. Finally getting the door opened, she turned to thank him for the evening.

"I've always heard you're not supposed to mix business with pleasure, but I sure did it tonight." Pam held out her hand.

But he didn't take it. He put both his hands on her shoulders, slowly moving them down her arms and around her waist, finally pulling her against him. Before she could find the strength to resist, his lips were on hers, and she was helplessly responding.

She felt his heart racing against hers, the warmth and roughness of his face was lost in the wondrous scent of him. And the last vestige of anything resembling a thought vanished.

Abruptly released, Pam was gently pushed inside. The door was closed. Then Cole was gone. She stood there, rooted to the spot, tracing her lips with her finger, listening to the sound of his car growing fainter.

Why was she feeling so confused, so disoriented? Because she wasn't used to men like that, she told herself. She was used to men like Alan, easy and comfortable.

But she'd learn, she thought with a resolute toss of her auburn curls. From now on, she'd be better prepared to hold her own with this smooth, experienced man.

Boss, she corrected herself.

CHAPTER FIVE

"The countryside is gorgeous this time of year," Pam remarked as Kate turned off the highway and slowly guided her Chevy along the dirt road that led to the shelter. "It wasn't this full of wild flowers last year."

"That's because there was so much rain in the desert this year," Kate explained. "All the guys and gals at Pet Haven are going to be surprised to see you so soon after your accident."

Pam glanced down at her cast. "It wasn't that big a deal."

As they drew closer, she could see the

end of the runs that projected from the big kennel behind the main house, and she felt the familiar tug of admiration for Madge Gerhardt, the rich widow who'd founded the program and turned it into such a successful operation.

"If Madge were president of this country," Pam murmured, "she'd have things under control."

Kate giggled. "She *is* the most organized person I've ever known, besides being a super saleswoman. She could have talked Ebenezer Scrooge into making a contribution."

As they passed through the entrance and approached the parking area, Pam spied Dr. Rolfe's station wagon. Which meant the vet, who donated his services every Sunday morning, was still inside the animal compound giving shots to the new residents who'd been rescued during the week, neutering those who were ready, and making routine examinations all around.

While Kate circled around, looking for an empty place, Pam whispered hastily, "No one here knows about the Farnsworth's job that came and went so fast.

So there's no point in going into it.
Okay? Or this new one at the restaurant,
for that matter. Time enough after I see
how it goes."

She'd already told Kate all about the
wonderful restaurant, the owner, and the
details of the interview. But she'd carefully omitted any mention of the date
last night. She wasn't sure why she still
wasn't ready to talk about that.

Kate pulled into a vacant slot, fluffed
out her long chestnut hair, and turned to
Pam with a conspiratorial wink. "My lips
are sealed."

They walked past the wing that
housed the offices—accounting, adop-
tion, newsroom—and on into Madge's
living quarters, where they were effu-
sively greeted by Madge's personal adop-
tees, Purrkins, the three-legged Siamese,
and big, shaggy Winthrop, the near-
blind collie.

Inside the spacious living room, which
had been filled with chairs, Pam was im-
mediately surrounded by all her friends,
having to explain, over and over, to this
one and that one, "I feel fine now... Yes,
I was very lucky... Yes, Alan will be

back next Sunday. He misses you all too."

A sharp rap of the gavel ended the socializing. Madge, a large, imposing woman, had assumed her place in the center of the room. "We have a big program today." Her voice was pleasant but authoritative. "So we'd best get right to it."

And the meeting began. There were the usual announcements. They all clapped when Madge named a well-known food manufacturer who had just pledged a weekly supply of canned and dry pet food. Finally the guest speaker was introduced, and Pam listened absently to the grim statistics about starving dogs and cats, a situation that could be alleviated by neutering.

She kept wondering how Cole Bradshaw felt about helpless, hungry animals.

When they left, Kate said, "I've got to make a quick detour to the shop, Pam. Yesterday was so hectic, I forgot my order forms. And I want to go over them tonight."

"I thought Ken was off this weekend.

Aren't you spending some time with him?"

Kate sighed. "He was called back to emergency today—that bus accident on Filmore. I'm paying the price of falling in love with a long-term med student. But..." Her face brightened. "He's got tomorrow off instead. I'm leaving my assistant in charge of the shop. We're going to the beach, and he specifically told me to bring you along, Pam. Even if you can't go in the water, you can get some sun."

"I've got nothing but free time," Pam said.

Kate pulled to a stop in front of the shop window that proclaimed in bold black letters: DOLLS—DOLLS—DOLLS.

As Pam followed her tall, willowy friend inside the store, she delighted as always in the sight of Kate's enchanted world of dolls—antique dolls, Cabbage Patch dolls, porcelain dolls, wooden dolls, Barbie dolls, all sorts of dolls imaginable. There were bins of miniatures, puppets, even pictures of dolls.

"I was never allowed to have a doll," Kate had confided once. "My parents wanted a boy, so I had to shoot baskets and build model planes with my father."

Now Kate's father was dead, and her mother was living in Phoenix with her second husband and his sons. Now Kate had a store full of dolls.

The week sped by in a flurry of activity.

Pam spent Monday night medicating her sunburn. Madge called Tuesday to tell her she liked her bookshelf placard and to ask if she could make another for the costume jewelry.

"And," Madge went on, "you and Kate did such a fine job with our fashion show last August, I'm hoping you two will collaborate on this year's. Farnsworth's is going to put it on for us this time. No big hurry, of course, but maybe you'd like to get started."

Pam said they'd get right with it.

Wednesday Kate insisted on leaving her assistant in charge of her shop again and going to the doctor's with Pam.

"We'll have lunch and do some shopping," Kate said, planning Pam's day.

"From now on, you're going to have to dress like the big career gal your new boss is counting on. Besides," she added kindly, "your wardrobe is long overdue for an overhaul, hon."

It was a thoroughly satisfying day. The doctor's news was all good. "You're a remarkably fast healer, Pam," he said after he removed the cumbersome cast and examined her wrist. "We'll keep it wrapped with this stiff little retainer for another week, and then we'll get rid of it altogether. And you'll be as good as new." His smile was encouraging. "In the meantime, I see no reason why you can't use that hand as much as you want to."

After a fortifying fruit salad in Farnsworth's tearoom, Pam let herself go, charging recklessly as she selected an expensive tangerine linen suit, two tailored dresses with becoming lines, a sharp plaid blazer, and blouses to go with her white slacks.

When she was home alone with all her new finery and added up the staggering bills, she told herself she really had to make good on the job now.

Another postcard from Alan came

Thursday. This time it was a picture of the Golden Gate bridge. This time the message was a scrawled: *See you Saturday night.* Pam looked forward to seeing him. She had so many things to tell him.

The long-distance call from Cole that night was reassuring. "Just wanted to make sure you haven't forgotten we're expecting you tomorrow," he reminded her. "I'll be back in town in time to make sure everything is ready for you. Will we see you around noon?"

"I haven't forgotten," she assured him. As if she could! "And I'll be there."

CHAPTER SIX

The next morning Pam dressed carefully in her new tailored jade-green dress with its matching jacket. When she pulled her Honda into the almost empty parking lot at a quarter to twelve, she experienced a fleeting sense of deja vu. There were differences, though. The Datsun was missing, which meant Art wasn't here yet. *She* was different, not nervous in the apprehensive, sweaty way, not lugging the portfolio with her samples and her hopes. Now she belonged.

As she started toward the building,

she saw Cole waiting in the open doorway with a pleased smile.

"You're early," he said. He was casually dressed in pale-gray slacks and a
plaid jacket, but not too casual to greet
the well-groomed dinner guests.

"So are you," she responded, then suddenly wondered if he was. She still didn't
know the schedule. "Or are you?"

He reached for her good arm and
guided her inside, letting the door swing
closed. Then his eyes widened as they focused on the new, smaller cast on her
other arm. "Hey, you've been to the doctor!"

She nodded. "It's almost healed. In another week I won't have to lug even this
one around."

"I'm glad." The smile returned. "In answer to your question, I open up when
I'm in town. When I'm up north, Jerry
gets here early. The hours for the crew
are staggered, depending on when
they're needed. As for you, Pam, noon
was an arbitrary shot." They were moving through the big empty kitchen.
"Jerry will have a key made for you, so

you can come and go as suits your purpose."

He was telling her again that she was on her own. But even Kate, who worked on an informal basis with her assistant, wasn't this loose. Pam shrugged. She was just going to have to be very careful not to take advantage of all this freedom.

As they approached the doorway to his office, Cole's hand took hers. "Here you are," he announced.

Pam stood still, speechlessly gazing into what had been the boss's office, finally expelling the protest, "But this is your office."

"Not anymore," he chuckled.

She kept staring around in stupefied amazement. Now there was a big artist's drawing board with a long-necked adjustable lamp attached to it and a high professional chair in front of it. One wall was lined with a built-in cabinet of drawers and open shelves that were filled with art supplies of every description. A new desk and swivel chair were flanked by two small leather chairs.

"For consultations," he explained, fol-

lowing her gaze. When she couldn't get
her voice past her swelling dumbfound-
ment, he asked anxiously, "Is everything
here? If we missed anything, just holler."

"It's beautiful," Pam breathed, moving
over to the shelves. "But what became of
your office?"

A phone rang, and he ducked around a
new partition. "Be right back."

Pam was staring at the labelled stacks
—poster boards in every size and shade
imaginable, reams of textured and tracing paper. Curiously pulling open the
drawers, one after another, she found
every conceivable tool of her trade. It
was as if somebody had bought out an
art-supply store. She felt like Alice in
Wonderland.

"Come and look at my new office."

Pam whirled around at the sound of
Cole's voice. He was watching her from
the edge of the partition. With a dazed
smile, she walked toward him and
peeked around the new alcove. It was
empty except for the massive desk that
dwarfed it.

"Now that I've been demoted," he said
good-naturedly, "I'm counting on you to

let me eat my dinner in your office."

Before Pam could wonder about that, he was pulling her back into her section. "Now how about leaving your purse and jacket in your own office and letting me give you the grand tour?"

She felt like a short-circuited robot as she let him take her jacket and purse and lead her back down the hallway. But as she followed him from one room to another, her interest in the well-oiled, behind-the-scenes efficiency of this establishment absorbed all her attention.

"There is where we take in our daily deliveries and store the surplus," he told her as they entered two adjoining pantries, each equipped with wide, double doorways, each opening out into a rear service area. "The larger room accommodates the restaurant's needs, the smaller one beyond taking care of the bar."

"I didn't dream there was so much space back here," she kept saying as they moved from one cubicle to another.

He showed Pam the cleaning crew's bailiwick, full of janitorial equipment of every description. "They come in every night at midnight," he said.

Then there was the maintenance room. "I see the painters left a lot of their supplies," he mused to himself. To Pam he said, "This is where we keep a few tools for minor repairs."

The large linen room had its own service entrance. Cole opened one of the cabinets to show her the stacks of clean linens, the huge hampers where they dropped soiled items for the laundry pickup.

When he saw her eyeing the ironing board and piggy-back washer-dryer, he said, "For small emergencies. And the clean uniforms are kept here." He indicated the rack where they hung in their cellophane bags.

When they came to two closed doors, one marked GUYS, the other GALS, he apologized, "Ladies aren't allowed in this side, and I'm not allowed in here." His smile crinkled the corners of his eyes.

That was when Pam noticed that they didn't look so blue today. Gray wasn't his best color, she decided absently.

"But that's where our people have their lockers, dressing rooms, lavatories, eating accommodations," he was saying.

"When the girls get here, they'll show you through their quarters." At the sound of squealing tires, Cole added, "That's Art. I've got to ask him about an illegible message he left on my desk. Why don't you wander around a bit, Pam?"

It was later when Barbara, the pretty little cocktail waitress, took Pam through the door marked GALS.

"We're all glad Cole hired a lady for this job," Barbara confided. "It makes us females a little less of a minority around here."

By that time Art and his two main assistants were busy in the kitchen and Cole was in Jerry's office conferring with him about the last-minute cancellation of a big wedding party.

The waiters, busboys, and waitresses had drifted in. Chicken International was coming alive. Pam's presence had been politely acknowledged by the manager, and she knew she hadn't imagined his coolness last Saturday.

She gave Barbara a rueful smile. "I'm glad somebody wants me here. I'm afraid Jerry doesn't."

"Jerry and Max Enright are personal friends," Barbara said absently as she squeezed herself into her skimpy uniform. "It could be Jerry blames you for Cole's taking the advertising away from the Enright Agency."

That would explain it, Pam thought as she drifted slowly back to her office, thankful everybody else had been friendly.

Cole was waiting for her. Already seated in one of the chairs at her desk, set now with mats and napkins and silverware, he was sipping a glass of Scotch. Savory aromas and familiar noises were sifting in from the kitchen, reminding her she hadn't had any lunch.

Rising and pulling out the other small chair for her, he said amiably, "Art's got the Chicken Creole from Haiti almost ready to go, so we're stuck with that tonight." He chuckled as she sat and he reseated himself. "Sooner or later you'll sample all our combinations." He took another sip of his drink. "And get used to this early dinner hour."

"I can't believe it's five already," she marveled. Where *had* the afternoon gone? "Don't the others eat here?"

Cole said, "Of course. Their dinner breaks are staggered throughout the evening."

"And they eat whatever we've got too much of," Art muttered and he wheeled their dinners in on a serving cart.

While he transferred the fruits of his labor—heaping plates of baked chicken swimming in a seasoned sauce of tomatoes and okra, a basket of hot buttered rolls, two bowls of fruit salad—Pam said fervently, "If you cooked it, Art, I'm sure whatever they get is delicious."

The chef smiled his thanks and left.

"Try it while it's hot," Cole suggested.

It was all the encouragement Pam needed. Picking up her fork, she dove in. She was so engrossed in appeasing her hunger pangs, she didn't notice Cole's silence until she looked up and saw how intently he was staring at her.

"For such a little girl," he teased, "you

sure pack it away."

"I'm still growing," she retorted, not wanting to admit she hadn't eaten all day. It might sound like a complaint. But she made a mental resolve to reorganize her meal routine to accommodate this new schedule.

From where she sat with her back to the doorway, she saw Cole glance past her and hold up his hand. Instantly one of the white-smocked busboys—Roy, she found out later—came in and cleared their table, then set down cups and saucers and a silver pot of coffee.

"Let me," Pam offered, reaching for the pot and pouring. "It's the first useful thing I've done all afternoon. But when we finish here, I'm going to make up for lost time."

"You'll get your chance tomorrow." He helped himself to sugar. "We'll go over the recipes we haven't tried yet, and you can help me decide which two to substitute. And, if there's time, maybe you can come up with an idea for a thirty-second radio spot we're thinking of running."

"Why can't we do the recipes now?"

she suggested. "I could look them over, and—"

"How's your head?" he interrupted, the lazy smile gone, the eyebrows pulled together.

Her right hand flew up instinctively. Her bangs were still covering the bruise. Had they blown away? "It's fine," she mumbled. "Now let's discuss the recipes."

"Now I'm going to send you home." He stood. "This was orientation day, remember? And I want you bright-eyed and bushy-tailed tomorrow."

She heard the finality in his voice and knew there was no use arguing. Her day here was over.

Before she could cross the room, he handed her her belongings. "I'll walk you to your car, Pam."

They were in the corridor when Jerry stepped out of his office. With a frosty nod for Pam, he turned to Cole. "The Abernathys have just arrived with Ben Grossman from the bank. They're waiting in the lounge for you."

Pam felt Cole's hesitation. With a toss

of her chin, she said quickly, "I can find my way."

Without a backward glance, she hurried away, through the now active kitchen, through the pretty, readied dining room, through the early diners congregating in the lobby, and out to the parking lot, all the while keeping the niggling doubts at bay.

Don't try to sort it out till you get home, she kept telling herself.

CHAPTER SEVEN

As soon as Pam was inside her apartment, she faced all the disturbing questions. Why had Cole had the biggest and best part of his own office converted into such an elaborate, well-equipped studio for her? Why hadn't he cared that she hadn't accomplished a single thing all day? She still wasn't exactly sure what she was supposed to do. Go over the recipes with him, he'd said, then mentioned a thirty-second commercial. Since when did a restaurant hire someone to do such things on a full-time permanent basis?

She tried to remember the duties he'd enumerated the day he'd hired her. The new menus, of course, and a different design for cocktail napkins and matchbook covers, ads, changes in the general decor. Did that add up to a real job?

Even the quick, easy way she'd been hired suddenly struck a false note. At the time she'd been too anxious to get the job to wonder why there hadn't been any application to fill out, why there hadn't been any competition for such a desirable spot. Just like that she'd been hired! Now it seemed too good to be true.

Like a snowball careening downhill, the doubts gathered momentum. All that special attention she'd been given last Saturday night seemed suspicious today —the lavish dinner, the extravagant compliments, the leisurely confidences.

Could all that really be his policy to make his new employees feel comfortable? And what about today, being escorted around as if she were visiting royalty, not allowed to lift a useful finger?

Bypassing the kitchenette, Pam moved

sluggishly into the dressing room and began one-handedly unzipping the back of her new dress.

Don't borrow trouble, her father had told her when she'd kept fretting over a test she was sure she'd failed. Was that what she was doing now? Because she was so used to pressure, deadlines, orders?

Pam hung up the green dress and reached for her cotton duster. She wanted the job, didn't she? She shook her head stubbornly. Okay, so she'd be a self-starter. She'd stop brooding about the laid-back scene and make herself indispensable. She'd do the job she was hired for even if it meant goading the boss into letting her earn her salary. Even if she had to remind him he'd promised to go over the new recipes with her tomorrow.

"What have you got against Chicken Cacciatore?" Cole asked Art. "We don't have Italy represented here."

The three of them were in Pam's office, Cole's father's recipes spread all over the table. It was her first conference, and she listened intently to the discussion between Cole and his head chef.

"Cacciatore's served all over town," Art said stubbornly. "The customers who come here expect something offbeat. Besides, this recipe calls for a side of spaghetti, and we're known for our varieties of rice." He paused, waiting for Cole's argument.

But Cole only shrugged. "Then how about that tarragon number from France?"

"Calls for noodles," Art objected.

Anxious to make a contribution, Pam said tentatively, "The Chicken Kiev from Russia might work."

Both men gave her a surprised look, as if they'd just remembered she was there.

Cole rallied first. "Good idea, Pam," he said heartily, too heartily. "What do you think, Art?"

Pam felt patronized. But maybe she was being overly sensitive. After all, it was only her second day, too soon to be important to the policy making.

"You about ready to tie into the payroll, Cole?" Jerry called from the doorway.

Cole pushed his chair back. "You two work it out," he instructed them. "I've got to give Jerry a hand now."

As soon as he'd disappeared, Art said, "I like your suggestion, Pam." He was studying the notes. "It's got all the right ingredients. We'll use it. Now we need another substitute."

Together they carefully examined each one of the entrees, Art wanting something unusual but without having to add any hard-to-get ingredients, Pam somehow feeling more involved. They finally agreed on the Szechwan Chicken with Cashews.

"I'll be surprised if that one isn't a big hit," Art said.

"I'll make copies of the recipes for you," Pam offered.

As soon as Art left to get started with the night's fare, Pam went to work making copies, one for Art, one for herself. Then, after slipping hers and one of the menus into her purse for later perusal, she went to work sketching out cartoon-like figures to represent the countries described in the menu.

She didn't see Cole again until he came in to join her for dinner.

"Chow time," he announced pleasantly, carrying his glass of Scotch. "You and Art get the new menu lined up?"

Pam left her drawing board and joined him at the table. "We decided on the two new entrees, but there's more to it than that. Anyway, we chose the Kiev from Russia and a great-sounding dish from China."

"China?" He frowned. "But we have one from there. There were plenty of other countries."

"Art said the one we already have is popular, though," she said. "And this new one is completely different. Besides, Art said it's from a remote area of China. And a lot of people are interested in Szechwan food." She rambled on about having to do some research to find some little-known amusing territorial facts. "And," she rushed along, "I want to make sure all my illustrations are appropriate."

"Take it easy, Pam." Cole's smile was

indulgent. "This is only your second day."

Before she could tell him it was high time she started accomplishing something, one of the busboys came in to set their table. Then Art was wheeling in a cart laden with tempting goodies.

"Pakistan tonight," he announced dourly. Then to Cole, "Pam tell you about our selections?" When Cole nodded, he asked, "Okay with you, boss?"

"Sounds great," Cole said agreeably.

When the chef left, Cole heaped her plate with a wry, "I hope you like chicken, Pam. Heaven knows you're going to be stuck with it one way or another five days a week."

"I love it," she said, tasting a juicy piece, "especially the delicious ways it's served here."

While they ate in companionable silence, Pam wondered uncomfortably if Cole was humoring her or if she just wasn't used to being on such cozy terms with her boss.

"I have another idea," she said finally. His thick brows rose questioningly, and she plunged in. "What would you think of running an ad in the entertainment section of the Sunday paper to introduce our two new dishes?" Encouraged by the approval in his eyes, she added, "I could work up an attractive layout."

"I think you have a great idea," he said enthusiastically, his eyes going so soft with surprise and approval, she had to lower hers. "In fact," he went on, "when we close up here tonight, I could drop over and we could discuss it."

The feeling of confusion swamped her again. Why did they have to discuss it in her apartment? Because there were so many interruptions here? Or because this was Saturday and she wouldn't see him again until next Friday? But they wouldn't be ready to serve the new dishes for a little while, anyway.

"I wish we could," she said carefully, "but I have a date with my friend, Alan, tonight. I could have a rough draft ready for you Friday, though."

"Alan? He the boyfriend who's been out of town or whatever?"

She flushed. "Well, he's more of a friend, actually." After all, Alan did not return the new warm feelings she'd been having about him.

Cole chuckled. "I wonder if he feels like just a friend."

"I assure you he does," she laughed.

CHAPTER EIGHT

Pam wasn't laughing that night when Alan asked her to marry him.

Her slightly built neighbor and friend had been waiting for her with a six-pack of beer when she got home. And right away she'd had to explain the cast on her arm. They were on seconds by the time she'd related her sad story with the happy ending.

When she'd asked him about his vacation, he'd described his two weeks in San Francisco and admitted ruefully, "But I guess I've planted my roots here now."

Then he took a deep breath and plunged in. "I'm not going to pretend I'm in love with you, Pam, the way I was with Eleanor. And I know you aren't in love with me that way, but..." His voice gave out for a moment. "Anyway," he pushed on, "we do like each other, and we do have so much in common, I don't see why we couldn't have a happy, worthwhile life together."

"That wouldn't be good enough for either one of us, Alan," she whispered, reaching for his hand, wishing his feelings for her could be deeper, stronger. "The right woman for you will come along, Alan." She groped for words. "But I do value your friendship. Can't we just keep on the way we are?"

"Sure." There was a mixture of relief and disappointment in his crooked smile. "Try, try again, if at first you don't succeed—isn't that what they say?"

Pam managed a wan smile with her nod. "But when you find that right girl, Alan," she said gently, "you won't have to ask twice."

He stood, then bent down to give her a

feathery kiss on the cheek. "I still like you better than anyone I know right now, friend."

"The same goes for me," she said fervently. If only he knew how much she liked him!

The next afternoon Pam rode to the Pet Haven meeting with Alan and turned in her latest contribution. Afterward, after everyone had made a fuss about having Alan back, they stopped off for pie and coffee. Alan's proposal wasn't mentioned, to Pam's great relief.

Monday she and Kate got together for lunch to discuss possible themes for the upcoming fashion show. Pam spent the rest of the afternoon in the library, taking copious notes from the reference books and lugging home several volumes.

She was up late that night writing the copy for the two new entrees, and she worked in her new office all Tuesday afternoon on the sketches. With a late, hearty breakfast under her belt, she didn't realize it was time for dinner until Barby popped into her office.

"Since the boss is out of town, we thought you might like to eat with us," she invited.

Pam accepted eagerly, anxious to make friends with the crew.

"I'll tell Art," Barby said, glancing curiously at Pam's cast. "What's wrong with your arm?"

Pam explained the accident, then shrugged it off with a casual, "But except for the temporary inconvenience, it's nothing."

"That's good." Barby edged toward the door. "See you in our lounge in about fifteen minutes then."

Besides Pam, there were only two of them, Barby and a friendly, exceptionally pretty girl named Diane. While the two girls exchanged cracks about an inebriated customer, Pam couldn't help noticing the differences in the service...Like a busboy doing all the honors, instead of Art, with an ordinary coffeepot instead of a fancy one, with paper napkins replacing the linen ones brought in for her and Cole. Not that it mattered! It just made Pam more acutely aware of her executive position here.

"Patty and Lynn eat their dinner when we go back on duty," Diane explained.

"But they're as curious as we are about your date with Cole," Barby confided while they all dug into the Chicken Creole. "We've all got a crush on him, but none of us ever got to first base."

"Of course, he's always been real nice to all of us," Diane wanted Pam to know.

"Anyway," Barby went on, "we'd all decided he probably had a special girl in Los Angeles." She paused, and Pam saw the look they exchanged. "Until Saturday night when he took you to dinner," Barby finished.

Pam felt a swelling horror at the gossip that had evidently been going on all this time. "For all I know," she said indignantly, "he probably does. Certainly he has no personal interest in me. That dinner was purely business."

Both girls looked crestfallen, but Barby didn't give up." "Even so, you must have gleaned some inside information on his love life."

Pam flushed guiltily as she remembered Cole telling her he was single. And no prospects, he'd said that night.

"Not only did we not discuss our personal lives," she said stiffly, justifying the lie on the grounds the truth was none of their business, "but I have no curiosity about his love life. My only interest in Mr. Bradshaw is as an employer." Even as she spoke, though, the memory of his kiss that night sizzled through her.

"Rumor has it we're changing our menu," Diane said, changing the subject.

Pam smiled gratefully, but it was suddenly dawning on her that she was walking a tightrope. Not sure if she should be contributing to the grapevine, she played it safe. "I couldn't say," she said lightly.

When the half hour was up, Pam drifted back to her office with the uncomfortable feeling she wasn't making friends fast. She knew it for sure after she was reseated at her drawing board and Jerry came in.

With a supercilious smile he laid a key

on her desk and glanced at his watch. "You're to leave by six o'clock, Miss Harper. Boss's orders."

She'd had it with this unfriendly man. "Thank you for reminding me, Mr. Crandell," she said coolly.

He strode out, and she put her work away. Here, at least, she told herself irritably, was one definite rule.

On the drive home she tried to shake off her depression. After all, her career was her first priority, not her popularity with her co-workers. And she got along fine with the boss. She'd just do the best job she could and mind her own business.

CHAPTER NINE

Pam got to the restaurant early the next day, determined to finish the drawings, and now that she had her own key, it didn't matter that no one else would be there to let her in.

Closed up in her office, she was so engrossed in her work, she scarcely noticed people coming and going until Diane knocked timidly on her door.

"Time to eat," she said when Pam opened the door. "We're hoping you'll join us again."

"I'd love to." Pam smiled, suddenly

aware of the activity all around her and surprised at how relieved she was that the girls weren't mad at her for her standoffish attitude yesterday.

It was pleasant and friendly. There was no mention of Cole or the menus or Pam's work. The conversation revolved around Harv's goof with one of the orders and the new man in Barby's life.

When Pam left at six, she was pleased with her progress—and the fact that she hadn't had a glimpse of Jerry all day. She was sure he was avoiding her despite Cole's saying she'd be working with him during his absence.

But she didn't need Jerry's approval, she reminded herself as she sailed through the restaurant, and everyone else—the waiters and busboys and maitre d'—sent her off with friendly words and smiles. That night she drove home feeling as if she really belonged at Chicken International.

At the doctor's the next morning Pam was totally divested of a cast. Thursday she took her nearly finished work home with her. And by the time Cole got back

on Friday, she had the new menu ready
to show him.

First he noticed the absence of the
smaller cast. "You really are okay now?"
His eyes flicked up to her forehead, back
to normal now too.

Assuring him she was as good as new,
she handed him her finished work.

His eyes shone with approval as he
studied the sample menu.

When he looked up, his praise was extravagant. "This sure is an improve-
ment," he said. "But how did you ever
get it done so fast? Could we ever use a
gal like you at the Los Angeles branch!"
He scanned through her rough draft
again. "I want to get this to the printer
right away."

He disappeared around the partition,
and Pam sighed ecstatically. There was
no mistaking his pleasure at her drawings. She was making good beyond her
wildest dreams.

She'd started sketching out an ad for
the new entrees when he came back.

"They're giving us a rush job on the
menus," he told her. "Now I'm going to

see how soon Art can have the two new recipes ready to be served. Then we'll see about working up an ad." He took off again.

We'll, he'd said. Just as if they were partners! Pam began doodling as her thoughts wandered. She was glad she'd made copies of the new recipes for Art. He'd said they had all the right ingredients. So it could go fast now...She shivered at the prospect of working with Cole on the new ad. Then she wondered if he did have a girl in Los Angeles, if the "no prospects" remark had been a line. He must have a girl! He was too attractive and virile not to have somebody. And if it was anybody here, those nosy waitresses would know about it.

Pam wondered who that girl was, how serious they were, if she worked for Cole. He had a condo up there, he'd told her. He drove a Jaguar. He had a whole life up there.

But he wished they had somebody like her.

"We're all set," Cole said excitedly when he came back. "Art can have them both ready a week from Sunday." He began figuring out loud. "This is Friday. We'll get the ad in next week in time for Sunday's paper. So let's put our heads together."

"Right." Pam gathered a sheaf of paper and a handful of pens, then put one of the extra copies of the new recipes on the table as she sank into the chair Cole held out for her.

He grinned down at her. "I could give you a big hug and kiss for this, but I heard somewhere you're not supposed to mix business with pleasure."

She flushed, wishing she hadn't said that. But did she want a kiss and a hug? "What would you think of something like: CHICKEN INTERNATIONAL INTRODUCES TWO EXOTIC NEW ENTREES?" she asked to cover her confusion. "Or, instead of INTRODUCE, we could say ADDS TWO EXOTIC NEW ENTREES TO ITS UNIQUE MENU. Then follow with the description."

"Yeah," he agreed slowly, "headed with our logo."

They worked together all afternoon, finally coming up with copy they both liked, barely getting their table cleared before the busboy came in to set it up.

"I've been eating in the lounge all week with Barby and Diane," Pam said.

His eyebrows lifted. "But not tonight, I hope."

She smiled at his concern. "It's just that I don't like to eat alone."

"Neither do I," he said. "So it's okay when I'm out of town. But when I'm here, you're stuck with me."

She felt secure enough to pretend to be offended. "Is that an order, sir?"

"Of course not." His smile was sheepish. "I just hoped you'd rather eat here with me."

"I would," she admitted shyly.

When Pam walked in Saturday morning, Cole was sitting in one of her chairs sipping a glass of orange juice. "I've got a favor to ask," he greeted her.

"Shoot." She put her purse on one of the shelves, fluffed up her hair, and took the chair across from him.

"The fact is my mother is the major stockholder here," he began. "She doesn't come in and interfere that way, but she does expect me to keep her posted on what's going on here." He waited, but when Pam didn't comment, he explained, "So naturally I told her all about you and what you've done for us."

Pam sat forward, suddenly alert. Now what? "Didn't she approve?" she asked anxiously.

His smile was reassuring. "On the contrary, she was impressed. And now she wants to meet you."

"She's coming in then?" Pam asked nervously, dreading another interview.

He shook his head. "She wants me to bring you out to the house for dinner Monday." He paused again. "I realize it's an imposition asking you to give up your day off, but ..." He let the rest of his sentence hang.

But this is an order from higher up, was what he meant. "I don't have anything else planned," she said, "so I'll be glad to go."

"Naturally, I'll pick you up. The thing is, the house is at the north end of La Jolla, right on the beach. So I usually go for a swim before dinner." He gave her a quizzical look. "So to save myself a lot of round trips, I'm hoping you'll be willing to spend a couple of hours at the beach with me. That means," he finished lamely, "picking you up around noon. We can shower and change at Mom's."

Pam was speechless. It sounded like the whole afternoon and evening. It sounded more like a date than business. But his mother did live a long way from her apartment. It made sense.

"Could we work it out that way?" he asked finally.

"I don't see why not," she said.

His smile stretched with relief. "That's settled then." He stood, suddenly all business. "Now I'll get going on my call to Mike Harris at the paper."

Alone in her office-studio, Pam shuffled through her list of things to do. But she'd lost track of what she'd planned to tackle next. Her mind was too full of this new development. Was it possible her ideas were so good he'd bragged about them to his mother? Was his mother really the boss, with Cole merely the figurehead?

Pam shook her head, trying to push the questions out of it. She'd find out soon enough now.

CHAPTER TEN

At five before noon on Monday Pam waited for Cole in a fever of excitement, her bikini underneath her zippered terry shift, her beach bag bulging with her makeup case and clothes for tonight— undies and her wrinkle-proof madras dress. The sandals she wore would have to do.

Cole arrived on the dot of twelve. "All set?"

"It just dawns on me you have the advantage," she said brightly, taking in his dungarees and wide-open shirt. "You'll

95

end up at home where you can get properly dressed."

"You look well prepared," he laughed, picking up the overstuffed beach bag. "But we're very informal."

"I sure hope so."

"This is our day off," he reminded her as soon as they were settled in the Mercedes, "so there'll be no business mentioned today."

Until his mother started quizzing her, she thought! But Pam refused to spoil the afternoon with that worry.

"We sure can't complain about this weather," she said.

"You ever been up to Los Angeles, Pam?" Cole asked lazily as he smoothly maneuvered the car onto the freeway.

"I've never been out of San Diego," she confessed. "Except once to Mexico." Her nose wrinkled at the memory. "But I've always wanted to go to Disneyland."

"Yeah, it's something to see all right. And you'd get a kick out of the Universal City tour where they demonstrate all the tricks of the trade. You know, when you see a movie of a ship capsizing in a storm in the middle of the ocean, it's really a toy model in a man-made pool of water with a lot of machinery simulating wind and waves. They show you all that."

"I'll add that to my list." She looked at him, but his attention was on the truck in front of them. He sounded and looked different, younger somehow, not like the successful executive who ran the most prestigious restaurant in town.

He passed the truck and turned to Pam, catching her stare and reaching over to give her hand a little squeeze. "I'm glad I talked you into this," he said softly.

"So am I," she whispered.

They settled into a comfortable silence after they left the freeway and headed north on the Coast Highway. When Cole finally turned left and pulled to a stop in the driveway of a white brick house with bright blue shutters, almost buried under colorful masses of pink oleander, Pam caught her breath.

"I thought we were going to the beach first," she protested.

"And so we are," he said calmly. "But we have to leave the car here and walk down the stairs."

He came around and helped her out. While he opened up the trunk, she looked down the long flight of wooden steps and saw the beach below, fenced on either side. It hadn't occurred to her he'd take her to a private beach. But why wouldn't he? This was a wealthy family. But she certainly wasn't used to such opulence.

"Ready?" He took her hand as they started down the steps, holding a wicker basket in his other. "Picnic lunch," he explained.

She'd forgotten all about lunch. "You spend your Monday afternoon in comfort and style, don't you?"

"Only when I have company."

She wondered if that happened every Monday, but she didn't ask.

They were at the bottom before she realized she'd left her beach bag in the car. "I don't have my suntan lotion," she wailed.

He laughed. "We've got all that stuff." Pulling his key chain out of his pocket, he turned to a padlocked shed. "I've got all the necessities of beaching in here." She watched him pull out a blanket, huge towels, lotion, sunglasses. He held up a pair of surfboards and looked past her out at the horizon.

"No surf today," he muttered. "We won't need these."

"Waves or no, I sure won't," she retorted. "I don't know anything about surfing."

"Do you know anything about beach balling?" he asked, holding up an enormous red-and-blue ball.

"I can catch."

"But most girls can't throw," he teased.

"Tut, tut, that sounds macho," she teased back.

"Heaven forbid," he exclaimed in mock horror.

She helped him spread the blanket. Then they both stripped down to their swimsuits.

"Now," he said as he unscrewed the lotion bottle, "turn over, and I'll do your back."

She rolled obediently and felt a tingling all the way down to her toes as his fingers gently kneaded her shoulders, then slithered down her back. She hoped he couldn't hear the loud racing of her heart. By the time he got down to the backs of her legs, she felt as if she were dissolving.

"My turn," he said finally, handing her the bottle.

She returned the favor, marveling at the feel of his muscles and the narrow thread of blond hair that curled along his spine. As she massaged the scented lotion into his flesh, she felt as if her fingertips were on fire.

"You're well done now," she said abruptly. "And I'm hungry."

He sat up and reached for the picnic basket. "I hope you won't miss the absence of chicken."

She giggled. "I like chicken," she said loyally.

"Yeah," he agreed. "But today's the day of rest."

He spread a red-checkered tablecloth on top of the blanket, and, as he began unloading the basket, her eyes widened. There were ham-and-cheese sandwiches, a carton of potato salad, and a bucket of fruit—grapes and peaches and plums.

"I hope you like port." He lifted out a bottle of wine and a corkscrew.

"I like everything I see, but where's the army that's going to help us?"

"I've got confidence in you, Pam. I saw you in action Saturday night."

To her surprise, they not only finished it all, but she did her share.

"It must be all this fresh air that made me eat so much," she said defensively. "And now we can't go in the water for an hour."

"We can get our feet wet," he countered. He stood and held out his hand, pulling her up.

It was a magical afternoon. They splashed each other and skipped pebbles and tossed the ball back and forth and generally played like children.

When it was time to leave, she couldn't believe the afternoon had gone so fast.

"I have no right to feel the way I do about you, Pammy," he said soberly as they trudged up the steps.

She didn't say anything, but she knew what he meant. There was a chemistry between them that was as compelling as a magnet. Something different from her feeling for Alan. But any kind of romantic entanglement between them was impossible. They were, after all, employer and employee, and a personal relationship between them was unprofessional to say the least.

CHAPTER ELEVEN

As Pam and Cole approached the house, his big, strong hand was wrapped around hers. It was almost as if he felt her sudden jitters as the unsettling little worries began assailing her mind from every direction.

The gossip about Cole was already rampant, with the other employees speculating on his love life. And her own denial of knowing anything—or caring about him other than as her employer. Then there was Jerry's ill-concealed resentment of her. She shuddered. And her pretense about not knowing anything

about the new menus, when she'd been
actively involved with them from the beginning.

Now she was about to be scrutinized
by the restaurant's real owner. "Do the
waiters know about the new menus?"
Pam asked abruptly.

"Darned if I know," he answered indif-
ferently. "Didn't you mention it to the
girls last week?"

He didn't care. At least that was one
thing she could straighten out.

"We'll go in the side door," he was saying. "Then we can slip up the back stairs
and get cleaned up. Mom is probably at
her piano in the family room."

Pam followed him into a pretty, well-
appointed guest room and took her bag.

"Meet you in the hall whenever you're
ready," he said softly as he closed the
door after him.

Pam hurried, showering in the adjoining bathroom, doing her face and hair at
the vanity, bundling up her damp, sandy
stuff. Satisfied she looked as good as she
could, she steeled herself for the dreaded
meeting with her real boss.

Cole was waiting in immaculate white

cords, his damp hair slicked back. The frank approval in his blue eyes as they swept her gave her the courage to ask, "Will I pass inspection?"

"With a ten plus," he assured her.

He held out his hand, but Pam didn't take it. She didn't want Mrs. Bradshaw to get any wrong ideas.

It was Pam who had the wrong idea, though. As soon as she met Cole's sweet-faced mother, she felt herself unwinding.

When Mrs. Bradshaw said, "You're as pretty as Cole said you were, and I'll bet you're every bit as smart," she relaxed completely.

Cole officiated at the bar, serving orange coolers, telling his mother, "I promised Pam no chicken today."

The modishly coiffed silver-haired woman let out a tinkly little laugh. "Never on Monday." In a conspiratorial whisper to Pam, she added, "That's how I bribe my son to eat with me. He's crazy about shrimp salad. I hope you are, dear."

Pam said it was her favorite, and they chatted amiably for a few minutes while they sipped their drinks, Pam admiring the house, Mrs. Bradshaw asking her advice on the framing of a Picasso print she'd just acquired, Cole watching them both with affection.

While they were eating on the screened porch, the maid told Cole he was wanted on the phone.

As soon as he left, Mrs. Bradshaw said, "I'm so glad Cole wanted us to meet, Pam. Now I understand why he's been raving about you."

Startled, Pam dropped the blueberry muffin she was buttering, the thoughtless words blurting out of her: "He said you never came into the restaurant."

"Heavens no," Mrs. Bradshaw exclaimed, oblivious to Pam's confusion. "I'm happy to leave the whole business in Cole's capable hands. In fact, the less I know about it, the better I like it. Perhaps Cole told you I'm all wrapped up in my music."

Not waiting for Pam's response, she went on. "He's such a fine son." She laughed lightly. "Cole has an overdeveloped sense of responsibility. He's concerned with his employees' personal problems, and when my two sons were growing up, I could always count on him to look after his shy, smaller brother." Her eyes misted. "I guess you heard about our tragedy?" Pam nodded, and the older woman said, "Now Cole's still worried about Norm's grieving fiancee."

"Natalie?" Pam said.

Mrs. Bradshaw nodded. "She's such a sweet girl, very beautiful, but so shy, so frightened of everything. She can't seem to adjust to her loss."

When Cole came back, Pam remembered his mother's words. *He'd* wanted her to meet his mother, not the other way around. He'd wanted her to spend the day at the beach with him. He probably hadn't asked her for an out-and-out date because he thought she'd tell Barby. Or was he afraid she'd refuse? Was that why he'd pretended it was business? The main thing was he'd *wanted* to spend the day with her, and she was flattered and thrilled.

When it was time to leave and Pam thanked her hostess, Mrs. Bradshaw said, "I hope you'll come again soon, dear. Perhaps next Monday?"

"I'd love to," Pam said. "If it's all right

with Cole." She looked up at him and was rewarded with his pleased smile.

On the drive back to her apartment, he slipped his arm around her. "You made a big hit with Mom. What did you two talk about while I was gone?"

She smiled to herself, resorting to a safe topic. "She said you worried about Natalie."

She thought it was a safe topic until she felt the tightening of his arm, heard the sudden heaviness of his voice when he said, "The poor kid's had a rough time of it. Her mother and younger sister were killed in an auto wreck when Natalie was only ten. Her father—he owns that big hardware emporium on Olive—took it hard, and ever since he's been overprotective of Natalie. Now she's afraid of her own shadow." His voice had thickened, finally trailing away.

Pam realized the subject was obviously painful to him, and she was sorry she'd brought it up.

But before she could find a way to change it, he withdrew his arm and added, "Poor Nat would have had a life of her own as Norm's wife, but—well, for his sake I'm trying to help her emerge from this crippling cocoon her father keeps her in."

They rode the rest of the way in silence, Pam settling back into her own misery. Her happy glow from the lovely afternoon and evening was gone, her foolish hopes dashed. She kept thinking of Natalie. Poor, beautiful Natalie.

When Cole pulled up in front of Pam's building, he got out and came around without a word. When he left her at her door, he broke the silence with a flat, "See you Friday."

Without a touch or another word, he walked down the stairs and disappeared into the night.

But he liked her work, she reminded herself. Suddenly, though, it wasn't enough anymore.

And what about Natalie? Was it possible Cole had fallen in love with poor, beautiful Natalie?

CHAPTER TWELVE

Pam spent that next week keeping up a happy front for Kate and Alan, working hard at the restaurant on some matchbook-cover designs, and trying to mend her fences with her co-workers there.

When Barby came in Tuesday to remind her it was time to eat, Pam snatched the chance to clear her conscience on the matter of the new menus.

"You were asking about the new menus," she began in a confiding whisper after the three of them were seated.

"Well, I found we are getting new ones—
with two new recipes and illustrations to
make them even more attractive."

Their surprised faces told her they
hadn't heard.

"I'll bet Cole got you to do the pictures," Diane exclaimed.

When Pam admitted it, Barby said
warmly, "I'll bet they're good. How soon
can we see them?"

By the time the half hour had ended,
Pam knew she'd thoroughly ingratiated
herself, and she was relieved they hadn't
brought up the subject of Cole's love life
again.

On the chance they might, she begged
off Wednesday on the pretext of running
behind schedule on the new matchcover
designs that were due tomorrow.

Thursday morning she inadvertently
was given another excuse when she
found a memo from Jerry on her desk:

*Cole phoned to have me tell you to see
Ed Fenwick at KCGL this afternoon to
see how commercials are done.*

Then it was Friday and Cole was back
—back, waiting for her in her office with
the old friendly grin and the approving

gleam in his eyes. And it was as if the sun had come out after a long, dark night.

"Everything okay around here?" he asked just as if she were second in command.

"Everything's fine," Pam said with a sudden spurt of confidence. Glowing inside, she told him about her visit to the radio station and her idea for a thirty-second spot for them. "And," she added, "I've finished those matchbook designs."

His face lit up. "Let's have a look at your latest artistry."

As Pam handed him the sketches, she breathed a deep sigh of relief. Whatever had gone wrong Monday night was all right now.

For the next few weeks Pam was happy and busy with her friends, Pet Haven activities, and her job. She'd even done a painting that was hung up in the female employees' lounge, a lovely watercolor. When she couldn't avoid the gossipy waitresses, she was careful to keep the conversation impersonal.

Happily, she and the disapproving Jerry kept managing to keep out of each other's way. When she was with Cole, she avoided the touchy subject of Natalie, and he couldn't have been more attentive. The Mondays at the beach and dinner with his mother became a taken-for-granted routine. Altogether it was a pleasant time.

By the first of August Pam knew she'd fallen in love with Cole. She was sure he felt the same about her. Sometimes she'd catch him watching her in a brooding way, his eyes dark with emotion. He'd come into her office on the flimsiest excuses, and his goodnight kisses when he left her Monday night were hungrier than ever.

The trouble was she wanted more than the Mondays and the two dinners a week at work. She wanted him to say the magic words: I love you.

"I think you've fallen in love with your boss," Kate said one night. "I recognize the symptoms."

They were working on the fashion

show in the back of Kate's shop. Pam looked up from the poster she was lettering, ready to make an indignant denial. But what was the point of trying to fool Kate?

"I guess I did," she admitted grudgingly.

"An attractive boss is a common pitfall," Kate laughed. "The lovelorn columns are full of these situations. If it isn't a secretary falling for her boss, it's a patient falling for her doctor."

"It's not funny," Pam bristled, resenting Kate's making a joke of it. "But I do think—I hope—he cares for me."

"Then why the long face?"

"Because he doesn't say it in so many words," Pam fretted. "And I never see him outside of work except for those Mondays. Once," she went on slowly, "in the very beginning, he wanted to come over Saturday night, and I said I had a date with Alan. He hasn't tried since."

"He will. You'll get another chance." Kate wasn't laughing now. "He's probably worried about stirring up a lot of gossip," she said sympathetically. "A romance between two people in the same workplace is generally frowned on."

"I realize that," Pam said, "but no one would have to know. No one knows we see each other every Monday. No one would know if he admitted he loved me," she added plaintively.

"If he is in love with you, hon, he'll want more too. Be patient. Don't push. That turns guys off."

Pam did get her chance, in a round-about way, that very next Saturday night.

She'd left work and, finding her battery dead, gone back into the restaurant to call a service station. But Cole had seen her and insisted on driving her home.

"Then I'll have my mechanic replace the battery Monday while we're at the beach," he told her. "And since you'll be driving to your meeting with your friend tomorrow, you won't need it."

"But Alan's tied up with a tutoring job," Pam remembered. "I could ask Kate to pick me up, though."

"What time does this affair begin—
and end?" he asked.

"We start at one, and it's usually over
by three."

"Good. I could be back here in plenty of
time." He took her arm and propelled her
back out to the parking lot. "I'll pick you
up and drive you out there."

He ignored Pam's spluttered objec-
tions, and by the time he had her tucked
into the Mercedes, she was too thrilled at
the prospect of seeing Cole tomorrow to
argue.

"I think you'll enjoy the meeting," she
said brightly.

"I'll enjoy being with you." He reached
over and picked up her hand, asking
where the shelter was. When she told
him, he said thoughtfully, "Then it'll
take a good forty-five minutes to get
there. Which means leaving at noon." He
turned for a quick questioning glance at
her. "I hear they have a pretty deluxe
brunch at The Seaside. Ten-thirty too
early for you, Pam?" His arm came out,
and she melted against him.

"It's my turn to feed you," she said

gaily. "Brunch at my apartment tomorrow at ten-thirty."

"Best offer I've had all day. But how do I know you can cook?" he asked with elaborate concern.

"Sometimes we have to take a chance," she answered pertly.

Retreating into her own thoughts, she began planning her menu. A fresh fruit compote in those cut-glass stemmed dishes her mother had left with her. Then little pork sausages rolled in pancakes. She could walk the block and a half to the supermarket tonight to get the supplies.

"Hey." Cole's voice came through insistently. "Where have you gone? I said, 'What can I bring?'"

"Just yourself," she said firmly.

CHAPTER THIRTEEN

Pam's brunch was a huge success, with Cole enthusiastically consuming everything in sight, with the basket of daffodils he'd brought lending an extra-festive touch to the counter.

When they finished, he patted his stomach and said admiringly, "There's no limit to your talents."

Pam flushed with pleasure.

They got an early start and were on their way before Pam remembered the letter in her purse.

"Would you mind stopping for a second at some mailbox?" she asked anxiously, waving the envelope she'd extracted from her handbag.

"Sure. Another boyfriend out of town?"

She looked at him sharply, wondering if she actually detected a note of jealousy in his voice. "No boyfriend here or anywhere. It's a letter to my parents. I got theirs yesterday from Maine when I got home last night. And since they're leaving at the end of the week for points unknown, I answered right away."

"It's got to get there next week, huh? Then maybe we'd better mail it near the post office." He made a neat U-turn and headed back to town.

A few minutes later he pulled up to the outside box at a sub-station and leaned out his window to read the pickup schedule. Satisfied, he took the envelope from her and dropped it into the slot.

"I suppose they know all about your accident," he said casually as he headed back to the highway.

"Now they do. But I didn't tell them anything until you hired me. I didn't want to worry them."

"Do you like the job with us as much as you would have liked the one at

Farnsworth's?" he asked, suddenly serious.

"There's no comparison." She sighed contentedly. "As Kate said, losing that job was a blessing in disguise. If I hadn't lost it, the agency wouldn't have sent me to you."

"Then I can't be sorry either," he said softly, slipping his arm across her shoulder.

It was nearly one when they pulled up to the Pet Haven entrance and Cole said, "I'll pick you up here at three."

"But aren't you coming in?" she gasped. Then, when he shook his head, she wailed, "But what will you do all this time?"

"Get reacquainted with the desert," he quipped. "I'm not a member here, Pam. So don't argue. Just think of me as your chauffeur."

She wanted to protest, to tell him anybody was welcome, but she recognized the finality in his voice and swallowed her disappointment.

With a forced smile, she walked inside. Don't push, Kate had warned her. Be patient.

And she *was* making progress, she reminded herself.

Madge was pleased when Kate handed her their completed presentation for the fashion show. Alan came in during Madge's pitch for donations.

When the program ended and Pam walked out with Kate and Alan, she hastily explained why Cole would be waiting for her.

"I'll admit I'm curious to meet him," Kate said.

"But there was no need for him to come back for you," Alan muttered. "You should have realized I'd get here eventually and could have driven you home."

Pam didn't know what to say. Certainly she couldn't tell him she'd rather ride home with Cole.

Luckily she was spared the need to respond. Cole was walking up to her, and she was introducing them all. Kate was friendly. Alan was stiffly polite. Cole was charmingly cordial.

"So that's the boyfriend," he said thoughtfully as soon as they pulled away. "What's eating him?" He chuckled.

"Tired of being like a brother?"

"You have it all wrong," she sighed. "Alan is hopelessly in love with a girl named Eleanor." Then she began telling him what had happened. She omitted the interval where she'd begun to feel something for Alan.

"The guy ought to be glad to get rid of a girl like that singer," Cole snorted when Pam finished.

"Why? She wanted a singing career, and didn't you say we all have to do whatever's necessary to reach our goals?" When he didn't answer, she added hastily, "You're probably right, though. I agree Eleanor wasn't right for him."

Cole sighed. "He isn't the only guy to fall in love with the wrong girl."

Now he was thinking about himself, Pam thought glumly. Because of their working relationship. Or was he thinking about himself and Natalie? Pam felt his withdrawal and didn't know what to do about it.

* * *

Pam's spirits lifted the next day when Cole picked her up for their afternoon at the beach.

"Got a favor to ask," he said while he took her arm to guide her down the stairs. "But I'll wait till we get to the beach to spring it."

During the ride out, while Pam kept up her end of the banter, she thought she'd burst with curiosity. She was so sure Cole had worked something out. Something important.

"I'd like you to go up to Los Angeles with me this week," he announced as soon as they were settled on the blanket. "Our eatery up there is barely holding its own, and I need your expertise to give it a lift."

Pam did a double take. Business had been the last thing on her mind. She couldn't make the transition.

"Maybe do some watercolors for the cocktail lounge, the way you did in the San Diego employees' lounge," he suggested. "You see, the layout is slightly different. There's more wall space. You'd have to look it over. And maybe figure out a more artistic arrangement of the plants. Or get some unique idea for an advertisement."

"You mean you want me to spend three days in Los Angeles with you?" she asked stupidly, while her thoughts nervously added up the nights—two of them. What was he really asking?

"I'll book a hotel room for you," he went on in a businesslike tone, apparently unaware of her dismay, "and make reservations for us on the nine-o'clock flight."

Ashamed of the thought that had whizzed through her mind, Pam recovered with a formal, "I have nothing scheduled this week I couldn't postpone."

"Good." His smile was warm. "And since you haven't been there before, maybe we can work in a little sightseeing."

Pam's excitement soared while she packed for the trip that night. Thank goodness he hadn't been aware of her first fleeting suspicion! It would be like a long date, even if they were there for business. And now she'd have a good chance to find out once and for all if he was involved with somebody up there. Somebody she'd never heard of. But she wasn't really worried about it. His kiss when he'd left her at her door tonight had been deliciously possessive.

When she went to bed that night she could hardly believe that in ten hours she'd be in Los Angeles with Cole Bradshaw.

Then she thought about poor, beautiful Natalie. She pushed the thought out of her mind.

CHAPTER FOURTEEN

Cole and Pam took a taxi from the airport to his condo in the Palisades. It was small, but it had every luxury—the open beam ceilings, the stone fireplace, the island kitchen.

"I think you'll be more comfortable here, Pam," he told her as he set her luggage down in the bedroom. "So I'll take the hotel room." When she demurred, he insisted. "I'm going to check in now. You have one hour to get unpacked. Then I'll be back, and we'll start having some fun."

He left, and while Pam wedged her

things into his overcrowded closet, she felt strangely exhilarated. Fun? Probably because it was too early to go to the restaurant.

They spent what was left of the morning driving around and making plans.

"We'll do Disneyland tomorrow," he decided, "and take the Universal City tour the next day. You'll get a kick out of the way those barroom brawls are faked, with nobody getting a scratch."

"But aren't we supposed to be at the restaurant?" she asked.

"Yeah." He shrugged. "We'll put in an appearance after lunch today and see if we can't get everything wound up this afternoon."

Pam didn't know what he meant by that when this was only Tuesday. But for all she knew, this could be the loose way he operated up here.

They ate at Pierre's sidewalk cafe on the Sunset Strip, and Pam was enchanted with the view of the huge, sprawling city spread out below.

The Los Angeles Chicken International was beginning to gear up for the five o'clock opening when they got there.

It was different from the San Diego branch, but it was every bit as glamorous. And the manager—Dave Somebody—was a lot nicer.

While he and Cole were closeted in his office, she wandered around, suddenly remembering her recurring need to find out about a special girl up here. If it was one of the pretty cocktail waitresses, it must be over now. Or had he brought her here to make whoever it was jealous? Or to show that girl he'd found somebody else?

While Pam made mental notes in the cocktail lounge for the watercolors she might do and for a more attractive arrangement of the foliage, she kept surreptitiously eyeing the girls.

They were all friendly, and while she chatted with two of the really gorgeous ones, she uncovered such unusual facts in their backgrounds she decided an interview-type ad with their photographs would be effective.

When Cole emerged and pulled Pam away, he said gaily, "I've cleared my decks here for a while. Now let's get on with our vacation."

She hid her delight behind a reproving, "Vacation? I thought this was a business trip."

He laughed, unabashed. "You got something against vacations?" He opened the door of the Jaguar. "Get in, and I'll show you how much fun vacations can be."

"I'm not complaining," she said happily. If they were going to take the day off, why should she object?

They drove through the imposing mansions in Beverly Hills, with Cole regaling her with anecdotes about Hollywood. It was twilight when they got down to a marina where they had a seafood feast. It was very dark when Cole deposited her back at the condo.

He unlocked the door and slipped the key into her purse. Then he pulled Pam into his arms and gave her a very businesslike kiss.

"Get a good night's sleep, Pammy. It takes a week to cover Disneyland, and we'll have to do it in a day."

"'But this is your place," she whispered. "Aren't you coming in?"

"I'm afraid to," he said simply.

"Of me?" she gasped.

"Of me." His voice was suddenly scratchy.

With a gentle push, she was inside, and the door was firmly closed.

Pam wandered around, too excited to go to bed. Staring at a framed family photograph, she realized the younger, smaller boy would be Norman, the older, balding man Cole's father. A wave of sadness washed over her.

In the bathroom she ran into Cole's shaving equipment and was touched at his consideration in putting her up here. In the bedroom she found an assortment of men's jewelry on the dresser, recognizing a tie clip she'd noticed in San Diego, and she imagined she felt his presence in the room.

When she did get into the big bed, it was still hard to close her eyes.

She tossed restlessly, finally falling asleep.

When the phone jarred Pam awake, a glance at the clock told her it wasn't quite seven.

"Wake up, sleepyhead," Cole ordered. "I'll be there in fifteen minutes. Be

ready. And for gosh sakes, wear something comfortable."

She hurried, but when he knocked on
the door, she rushed to open it in her
robe. "I'm almost ready," she apologized.

"I'll start the coffee," he said. She eyed
the paper bag, the bakery box he was
carrying. "Juice and danish," he explained. "Now scoot."

She flew out of the room, reappearing
fully dressed five minutes later and finding him setting the table. "I never realized you were so domestic," she teased.

"You think I'll make a good husband
for some lucky woman?" he said.

She stared at this new Cole in
sneakers and a loose sweat shirt over
denim bermudas. He was somehow different, freer, happier, somehow more
boyish.

"This'll tide us over," he was saying,
not waiting for her response. "It's a long
drive down to Orange County."

"I feel as if we're playing hooky," she
said with a stab of guilt. "Though I did
accomplish a lot yesterday." She told him
about the ideas she'd worked on yesterday.

"We'll discuss it some other time, Pam," he said impatiently. "Right now we'll have to get going with our well-earned vacation."

A funny new suspicion filtered through her mind. "But you said the restaurant here wasn't doing well," she blurted. "You said you needed me to give it a lift." Puzzled, she stared at him and saw the dark red stain blush up under his collar.

"I had to make sure you'd come," he said.

He'd tricked her into this. Because he wanted to be with her.

Any means to an end, he'd said. If it's a good end.

"I'm glad I came," she said finally.

His sudden smile was like a caress. "So am I," he said softly.

Twenty minutes later the sink contained some dirty dishes, and they were on their way. An hour and a half after that they entered the enormous park that was a magical fairyland.

They traipsed around like kids, hand in hand, in and out of the endless exhibits. Pam clung to Cole on the roller coaster. He nuzzled her in the tunnel of love. As they wandered here and there, they nibbled on peanuts and popcorn and chatted with Mickey Mouse. They bought souvenirs and panned for gold and finally ate dinner in an Old West Saloon.

Cole excused himself between courses to phone Dave at the restaurant. When he came back, he said happily, "Everything's going smoothly without me. But I'll keep checking in and hoping I won't have to go back this week."

He'd already arranged for this time off, Pam knew now, to show her a good time. Which proved she was important to him in a way that had nothing to do with her contribution to his business.

"What's next?" she asked eagerly.

"As soon as it's dark enough, you'll see a fireworks display that beats anything San Diego offers."

On the drive back, Pam kicked off her shoes. "I'm going to have to soak my aching feet if I ever expect to walk again."

"Then get soaking, girl," Cole advised, "because tomorrow you're going to have to walk all over Universal City."

Pam's feet did recover, and they carried her through an exciting tour.

"This place makes San Diego seem like a backward village," she said Thursday evening on their taxi ride to the airport. "It's sure fun to visit."

Cole said, "But you'd rather live in San Diego?" She nodded, and he went on softly, "Then so would I."

She looked up at him, sure her heart was in her eyes.

"I guess it's pretty obvious I've fallen in love with you, Pam," he said, pulling her closer into the curve of his arm.

But she heard a tinge of resignation in his voice, felt an odd reluctance in his kiss. Didn't he want to be in love with her? Did a part of him love someone else? Or was she borrowing trouble again?

Determinedly throwing off the worrisome doubts, Pam snuggled closer to him and whispered, "I'm glad. Because I've fallen in love with you, darling."

His kiss should have reassured her. And so should the fact that he didn't seem to have a girl in Los Angeles.

But a nameless apprehension persisted. How could she be sure?

Besides, didn't Natalie live in the San Diego area?

CHAPTER FIFTEEN

Pam's uneasy feeling deepened the next morning when she arrived at the restaurant and Cole greeted her with an admiring, "I always liked that suit on you, Pam."

"I've hardly worn it," she said.

"Jerry's having trouble with the payroll today," he went on, "so I'll have to give him a hand. See you later."

Pam opened her briefcase—a new accessory—to get the notes she'd taken in Los Angeles. Even though Cole hadn't taken her there to work on the restaurant, she liked her idea for the ad, and she wanted to work it up. And she intended to get started on the watercolors for the lounge. It would be up to Cole, of course, to decide if he wanted to use them.

But she couldn't concentrate. His remark about her khaki suit kept sneaking into consciousness. She hadn't worn it *anywhere* since the morning of the accident because of the grease stain on the skirt the cleaners hadn't been able to remove. This morning she'd decided the smear wouldn't show if she kept the jacket buttoned.

So Cole couldn't have seen it. Not on her! He must have seen it on someone else and got mixed up. That was it. Suddenly Pam felt better. Men were so vague about women's clothes.

Pam never did see Cole again that day. He got involved with his attorney on some tax problem, and, after eating alone, she slipped out unnoticed.

Her phone was ringing when she walked into her apartment.

It was Kate.

"I need a favor, Pam," she said. "It's Ken's birthday tomorrow, and we're celebrating at the Hotel Vanda for dinner, dancing, the works. The problem is we're doubling with Ken's best friend and his new wife, Marvella." She paused for breath, then rushed along. "I only met this gal once—that was at Ken's college reunion—and she's not only a beauty, but she wears clothes like a fashion model. Which she is! Believe me, next to her, I felt like a Salvation Army reject."

Pam was wondering where she came in for the favor, when Kate told her. "I need you to help me find a dress she can't top. So will you go to Farnsworth's with me in the morning before work?"

"You don't need me, Kate," Pam answered, "but I'll be glad to tag along."

It was eleven the next morning before they found *the* dress for Kate.

"You look like a queen," Pam breathed when Kate emerged from the fitting room. "That amber color is perfect for you. And you have the height to carry off that tunic effect."

"This is it," Kate decided, admiring her reflection as she turned this way and that before the outside mirror.

Twenty minutes later, her new dress

swathed in tissue paper in its impressive box and back in her searsucker suit, Kate asked Pam, "Do you have time for a cup of coffee?"

"My hours are loose," Pam told her.

They were heading for the tearoom when Mrs. Brooks, the woman who had hired Pam just before the accident rushed up to her. "Oh, my dear," she exclaimed, "I'm so glad to see you up and around. I'm so sorry we couldn't hold that job for you. I do hope you've found something else."

"Almost right away," Pam said, telling her where she was working, then introducing Kate.

After the three of them had chatted a few minutes, the older woman asked, "Did that man ever get hold of you?"

"Man?" Pam repeated blankly.

Mrs. Brooks said, "A deep-voiced male called us that Friday morning, two days after your accident, asking for you. When I told him you didn't work for us and explained why, he asked where he could reach you. Naturally, I refused to give him your home number. But when he said it was urgent that he get hold of you, I did tell him the Perlman Placement Service might be able to help him." She scowled worriedly. "I do hope I didn't do anything wrong."

"Of course you didn't," Pam assured her. "It was probably a reporter."

A moment later Mrs. Brooks took off, hurrying toward the elevators. Pam and Kate drifted into the tearoom.

"Who could the man have been?" Kate asked after they'd settled into a booth and ordered coffee and danish.

"It must have been somebody who saw that newspaper writeup about the accident and assumed I worked at Farnsworth's," Pam said thoughtfully. "The newspaper story mentioned the Farnsworth's job interview, I think."

Kate thought back. "But why did somebody—some stranger—try to reach you that Friday? For what reason?"

Pam shrugged. "I don't know." Then the frightful words spewed out. "That was the morning Cole called the Perlman agency with his request for a design coordinator."

They stared at each other in mute consternation, Pam's thoughts fitting all sorts of nasty little pieces into place. It could have been Cole. He could have read that story. But a busy man like that wouldn't have paid any attention to it unless he was looking for it. And a busy man wouldn't be looking for it unless he had some reason to.

"His mother said he had an overdeveloped sense of responsibility," Pam remembered out loud.

"You said there hadn't been any such job as you have now," Kate remembered, "before he hired you."

Pam pushed her pastry aside and, with swelling horror, admitted, "That first day when I had that awful lump on my forehead, Cole asked me how my head was." It hurt her throat to keep pushing out her voice. "But I had it covered with my bangs. I was so sure he couldn't have seen it."

"The newspaper story mentioned your concussion," Kate reminded her. "He could have read about it, you know."

Pam nodded. "But when he asked about my cast and I told him about the accident, he acted surprised. But maybe it was just that—an act."

They kept groping back, blurting out pieces that kept adding up into an ugly picture. It was Kate who remembered that Mrs. Brooks had said the deep-voiced male had said it was urgent.

"And she put him on to the Perlman agency," Pam said. "But this is all circumstantial. Cole isn't a liar."

Even as the defensive words spilled out, though, she was remembering again the night he'd said he believed the end justified the means.

If the means don't hurt anyone, he'd said. Suddenly she couldn't hide the tears that welled up in her eyes.

"Don't cry, hon," Kate said softly. "He isn't worth it. And what the heck? If he was guilty, he made it up to you, didn't he? And what do you care how you got the job. Any way you look at it, it was a big break."

"It isn't the job," Pam quavered. "It's—" She couldn't go on. It was the man. She couldn't bear to think of the man she loved as being so devious.

"Look, hon," Kate said brightly, "for all we know, it could all be a terrible coincidence. What you should do is tell him what happened. He'll see how it looks to you, and I'll bet you anything he'll have a good explanation for everything."

"At least," Pam sniffed, "I'd be able to tell if he was telling the truth—now that I know all this."

"Call me tonight, and we'll laugh together at our silly suspicions."

"Sure," Pam said, dry-eyed now and hopeful.

All the while she drove to the restaurant, rehearsing her speech, she kept searching for the most tactful words. As Kate had suggested, she'd simply tell him what happened, but she'd let him think it was Kate who suspected him of being the hit-run driver, that she was amused at the coincidences. She'd be alert to his reactions, though. After all, forewarned was forearmed, wasn't it?

Cole wasn't waiting for Pam the way he usually did, and she was at her drawing board, dabbling with the watercolors for the Los Angeles branch, when Jerry walked in.

"Orders from the boss," he said flatly with his stiff little smile. "I'm to tell you Cole was called to Los Angeles on an emergency. Seems the auditor found a serious shortage in their books. He expects to be back sometime tomorrow." He walked out without waiting for her to say anything.

She felt unreasonably let down, realizing she'd counted on Cole's reassurances. As it was, the suspicions continued to haunt her.

But that night when she was eating alone, Pam suddenly remembered that Cole would have been out of town that Wednesday. In Los Angeles. So, of course, he couldn't have had anything to do with the accident.

She clung to that thought all night. And the next afternoon at the Pet Haven meeting, she managed to whisper to Kate that Cole had been called to Los Angeles and she hadn't seen him.

"But it was just as well," she murmured, "because later I remembered that he would have been out of town that day of the accident. So he's clear."

"I'm so glad," Kate whispered back. "Talk about a million-dollar misunderstanding."

But that night in bed, Pam kept going

over and over it. If only she hadn't run into Mrs. Brooks. If only she could forget the whole thing. Why was she borrowing all this trouble? She was glad of one thing. She was glad she hadn't had a chance to make an issue of it with him.

She wondered if Cole was back in town now. She wondered why he hadn't called her. After all, he did love her. And he knew she loved him.

Was it possible he loved another woman as well?

CHAPTER SIXTEEN

"So even though it took us most of the night," Cole confided, "it was worth finding the discrepancy in the bookkeeping." Propped up on his elbow, he trailed his fingers through the sand. "I knew none of the guys up there could be guilty of cheating, but it was still good to find I was right."

Pam smiled wanly. He *was* so good. He did care about his people. "I'm glad it worked out that way," she murmured.

They were at the beach, sprawled on the blanket, already thoroughly oiled.

"You're getting a nice tan," he said approvingly with a studied look at the length of her.

She kept her smile, not saying anything, but thinking he looked haggard with weariness.

"What's wrong, Pam?" He sounded concerned. "You're so quiet today."

"I'm just tired. Madge kept Alan and me after the meeting to give us a lot of rush orders on changes she wants in the next newsletter. So Alan and I were up late reworking it." That was true, but it wasn't what was wrong with her. It was all the doubts Mrs. Brooks had innocently stirred up that had drained her.

"Maybe I should wait for a more auspicious time to give you the present I brought."

She nodded, knowing she couldn't accept anything from him, not when she was still so bogged down with such unworthy thoughts about him.

"Let's wait until I've had a good night's sleep." She tried to sound interested, but she couldn't pull it off.

"Too tired to race me to the raft?"

She nodded again, and, with a feathery

kiss on her cheek, he ran toward the water.

Pam watched him moodily, wishing she could be really sure, so sure she could stop brooding about it.

"Do you like that picture there, Pam?" Mrs. Bradshaw asked, pointing to a large portrait of Mr. Bradshaw over the mantel.

The three of them were in the family room, Pam and Cole showered and dressed, Cole at the bar mixing their before-dinner cocktails.

"I love it," Pam exclaimed, so impressed with the excellence of the painting she momentarily forgot her nagging problem. "I can't believe I never noticed it before."

"I had it in my bedroom," Cole's mother explained, "but I think it belongs up there." She smiled sadly. "Cole had it painted from a photograph and gave it to me for my birthday," she went on dreamily. "Cole took the whole week off to be here with me. It was a wonderful week."

"Are you two whispering about me?" Cole teased, joining them with the tray of drinks. "Cheers." He lifted his glass.

They raised theirs and sipped.

Then Pam said, "I almost forgot. I brought a little gift for your mother, and I left it in the car. Will you get it for me?" It was a lie, and she hated that. But she suddenly had to know which week Cole had taken off to be with his mother. And she not only wasn't ready to discuss it with Cole, but she wasn't sure yet she ever would be.

Cole left, and Mrs. Bradshaw said, "You shouldn't have done that, dear."

"It was just a trifle," Pam murmured, knowing now she'd have to think of a trifle to bring next week. "Let's call it a belated birthday gift. By the way, when *was* your birthday?"

When Cole's mother unsuspectingly named the date in June, Pam quickly figured back. It was the Tuesday before that Wednesday she'd had the accident. Then Cole *had* been here in San Diego all that week!

Pam was so shattered that she scarcely

heard Mrs. Bradshaw's chatter about all the nice things Cole had done for her that week.

He came back with a worried, "I couldn't find it, Pam."

"I must have forgotten to bring it," she said penitently. But it was all an unthinking part of her lie. Her whole mind was on the devastating fact that Cole had to be that driver.

While they ate, Pam kept lapsing into silence, trying desperately to justify his act. An arrest for drunk driving would have cost him the respect of his employees, maybe even the customers. And Cole was a good driver. But he must have been drunk that one time.

Such a scandal would have hurt his mother. And he had tried to make it up to her. He'd had no way of knowing then he'd fall in love with her. No wonder he'd admitted it so reluctantly.

I have no right to be in love with you, he'd said.

"I've got to get this girl home to bed," Cole told his mother during dessert. "She's falling asleep on her feet."

"You're working Pam too hard," Mrs. Bradshaw scolded her son. To Pam, she said affectionately, "Don't let that workaholic bully you, dear. You deserve a nice vacation."

Pam flushed guiltily. "I promise to be better company next week," she said, determined to forget and forgive.

But she couldn't leave it alone, and after another fitful night, she knew she couldn't accept it that way.

By the time she got to the restaurant that next afternoon, she was through playing possum. One way or another she was going to have to settle it.

Determined to learn the whole truth and take it from there, she marched into Jerry's office.

When he looked up with his cool smile, she said directly, "I know you don't like me, Jerry. Does it have anything to do with the Enright cancellation?"

A look of surprise replaced the smile, and finally she saw a grudging kind of admiration in his eyes.

"An honest question deserves an honest answer," he said slowly. He took a deep breath before going on. "When Cole sprang the news on me that day he hired you, I asked if he was dissatisfied with the Enright Agency. He said not at all, that his reasons for replacing them with you were strictly personal." He held up his palms, a slow smile coming. But the contempt was gone. It was warmer now, almost apologetic. "Look, Pam, whatever you two have going is none of my business."

Pam felt a rush of heat flooding her face. So that's what he'd thought all this time! That she and Cole had been having an affair, and Cole had made a job for her! For all she knew, Jerry could have thought she'd blackmailed Cole into hiring her. Naturally, he'd resented what he must have considered a kind of nepotism —at the expense of his friend.

"Thank you for being honest with me, Jerry," she said stiffly.

She walked out, seething. Back in her own office, she knew she couldn't stay. It didn't matter anymore that she loved the job. She loved her sanity more. And Cole had lied to her. He'd cheated her. Even if

she didn't love him, she couldn't work
with a man she couldn't trust. And she'd
never be able to trust Cole Bradshaw
again. The situation could drive a girl
crazy!

She fought tears all the rest of the afternoon and finally left before the dinner
hour. She couldn't face Art or even a
busboy. Not today!

CHAPTER SEVENTEEN

Pam drove around aimlessly, trying to get used to all the losses. She'd get another job. It wouldn't be nearly as good as this one, but this one had never been a real job, anyway. And somehow she'd get over Cole. She'd gotten over Alan, hadn't she? She had too much pride to carry a torch for someone who'd betrayed her.

She owed it to herself to have the satisfaction of telling Cole that she was quitting—and why! She shuddered at the prospect of getting through the next two days before she'd have the chance, but she would do it.

In the meantime she wouldn't tell anybody what had happened—not Kate or
Alan, certainly not anybody at the restaurant. She'd let Cole make up his own
lie for his employees and his mother. He
was good at that. Time enough after
she'd settled the score with him to tell
Kate the whole truth. She'd simply tell
Alan she'd decided to quit and look for
something else. If he asked why, she'd
say she didn't like it there anymore. And
that was the truth!

Cole was waiting for Pam in her office
with a wide smile and outstretched arms.
"I missed you like crazy," he said.

She sidestepped him, her face stony.
She saw his smile fade and leaped right
in with a quiet, "I found out you were
driving the car that day I was hit, and I
know now you created this job for me as
a kind of compensation." When she saw
the guilt clouding his eyes, she added de-
spairingly, "I guess I won't have to tell
you how I found out."

"I admit I was involved in that accident," he confessed miserably. His arms

dangled limply at his sides as he cleared his throat. "And I did hope this job would make it up to you for the one you lost. But that was all I wanted, Pam." Now he was pleading. "I didn't know I was going to fall in love with you. Which began to happen that day I interviewed you. Heaven knows I tried not to." He reached out for her again, and again she backed away.

"When I knew I was hooked," he went on thickly, "I hoped you'd never have to know. I just wanted to spend the rest of my life making you happy." His eyes were bleak. "And now you must hate me."

"I don't hate you, Cole," she said softly, suddenly feeling almost as sorry for him as she did for herself. "In fact, I'm grateful to you for showing me that the end doesn't really justify the means. In any case," she finished with a spurt of self-righteousness, "I'm satisfied that you've paid your debt, and now I'm leaving."

"You can't leave," he argued. "You've done a fine job here. The restaurant needs you."

"You must realize I can't stay here

under the circumstances," she said coldly.

His face filled with anger. "I thought you said you were satisfied I'd paid the debt." His voice was suddenly harsh, and this time he grabbed her. No matter how she struggled, she couldn't escape his vise-like grip. "I love you," he grated. "And I can't just turn it off. Can you?"

"Yes I can," she cried. She would! "I can't love a man I can't trust."

His lips ground into hers. "Look me in the eye and tell me you don't love me."

Her anger and frustration made it possible for her to look at him and say, "I don't love you anymore."

He let her go so abruptly, she had to grasp the desk to regain her balance. She was furious.

But the rage had drained out of him. "May I expect two weeks' notice?" he asked. "I'll need the time to find a replacement."

"With the understanding that our relationship from this point on will be strictly business." She had to struggle to keep her voice steady. "And I'll leave it to you to announce this change to your employees."

His lips moved, but no sound came out.

"If you do find someone before the two weeks are up," she said stiffly, "naturally, I'll leave then."

With a grunt he swung out.

Pam stood there, trembling and fighting tears. It was all finished now.

CHAPTER EIGHTEEN

The next day, the first of Pam's two-week notice, was even more unpleasant than she'd anticipated, with Cole barging in and out of her office without a word or a glance. She tried to work, but she felt an isolation that added to her heartbreak.

Cole didn't come near her at dinnertime, though he must have informed Art, who brought only one dinner in. She nibbled at the delicacy, thankful for her next two days away from the restaurant —and Cole. Two days, because she was sure there'd be no Monday date. Then, with a three-day reprieve while Cole was in Los Angeles, she might be able to face him next Friday. If he hadn't found her replacement by then! She prayed he would.

The next day at the Pet Haven meeting she managed to put on a light front of happiness. Luckily Alan's stint at the playground was almost over, and he was looking forward to the fall semester. Kate's mind was on a pending visit from her future in-laws.

But that night, alone in her apartment, Pam had to face the fact that it wasn't doing any good to keep telling herself she didn't love Cole anymore. The awful truth was that, whatever he was and wasn't, she was achingly in love with him. And she wondered how she'd get through the coming week, even with Cole in Los Angeles.

As it turned out, that week was fraught with unexpected upheavals. The first ghastly development was Cole canceling his three days in Los Angeles. Not that he bothered her! But he was *there*, not only there, but throwing his weight around in angry fits and upsetting all the employees. Though she only caught glimpses of him storming through her office, the gossip raged around her.

Tuesday it was Barby popping into her office. "Art said Cole is eating out with some studio mogul tonight, so I told him to have your dinner sent into the lounge. See you in ten minutes."

Pam had no choice but to join the girls.

"We're all wondering if Cole changed his schedule this week because somebody here's going to get the ax," Diane said while she helped herself to a generous portion of a Greek chicken concoction.

"I'm as surprised as you are," Pam said. And that was the truth. Unless, she thought privately, Cole was spending the week here to line up another artist.

"He's on the warpath, all right," Barby said. "He chewed Harv out for asking to reschedule his vacation. The poor guy just wanted to be free to help his wife when she gets home from the hospital with the new baby."

"Maybe it conflicted with somebody else's vacation," Pam said.

"Even if that was the reason," Barby said, "he didn't have to be so mean about it."

Wednesday it was the maitre d' waylaying her on her way out with a disgruntled, "What's eating Cole these days? When I told him a customer tried to pass off a stolen credit card, he told me not to bother him with details. He practically growled at me." The man shook his head in disbelief. "Yet those were my instructions."

"Maybe that's Cole's way of giving you more authority," Pam said soothingly.

Thursday she overheard a waiter complaining to another, "The boss sure is teed off about something."

Friday Pam was on her way to the rest room when she saw Cole bawling out a busboy for being rude to a customer.

Shamelessly eavesdropping, she stepped behind the wall and listened to the boy defending himself, to Cole cutting him off with an angry bark: "You're through here, kid. Pick up your paycheck from Mr. Crandell and get out."

Sick at heart, Pam scurried on into the

women's locker room. Would all this end when he found a new design coordinator? she wondered. But she hadn't even seen a sign of an applicant coming in.

Pam wondered if he had Mrs. Perlman lining up someone for the job. Or if he was doing his interviewing somewhere outside of his office. Jerry's, for instance! She couldn't see what was going on there.

Saturday, while Pam was putting the finishing touches to the pictures for the Los Angeles branch, she was painfully aware of Cole on the other side of the partition.

She couldn't help hearing him pick up his phone and dial, then his voice, tight and gritty. "If the next delivery isn't up to par, consider our contract canceled."

She cringed at the slam of the receiver. A moment later he barged out through her office and down the hall.

She sat there, trembling and wondering if a broken heart could be responsible for his uncharacteristic behavior. Or if he was mad at himself for trying to hide his guilt—from the authorities and from her. Or if he was mad at her for quitting! Or for being here! But that had been his idea.

Pam couldn't stem the rushing tide of speculations. Maybe he was so upset because this was his first failure and he couldn't deal with it.

She shook her head in an effort to shake away the endless, futile guessing. She just hoped and prayed he'd hire someone to take her place before she fell apart. Not only would she be better off, but so would everyone who worked here. If she had to stay another week, she hoped at least he'd be in Los Angeles for most of it.

Kate phoned Sunday morning to tell Pam she wouldn't be able to attend the Pet Haven meeting, because she was going to the airport with Ken to see his folks off. Pam was relieved. Her wound was still too raw to discuss it with anyone, even Kate.

She didn't have to put on an act for Alan either on the drive to the shelter. He was too preoccupied with some happy secret of his own to notice her glum face.

"I hope you don't have to go right

home after the meeting," he said mysteriously, "because I want to take you to The Seahorse."

"Why The Seahorse?" she asked curiously. The clandestine eatery up the coast was famous for its privacy, notorious for catering to romancing couples— and its outrageous prices. "You must have come into a fortune," she added. "Or you've heard from Eleanor." But why take *her* there?

He grinned. "It's a long story, and I can't get into it now. But I do want to tell you all about it. And The Seahorse is the most private place I know of."

Pam had never seen him so happy. His shoulders seemed straighter, as if a heavy burden had fallen from them. There was a new openness in his smile, a joyous lift to his voice. It had to be Eleanor.

But she didn't try to worm it out of him. She was too consumed with her own misery, just glad he was too preoccupied with his good news, whatever it was, to wonder about her state of mind.

* * *

The lowering sun was shimmering over the gently rolling Pacific when Pam and Alan were finally seated in one of the booths at The Seahorse, behind the drawn, beaded curtain with the iced teas and basket of fried clams.

"Now tell me. You've talked to Eleanor," she guessed.

He chuckled. "Yep. She made a surprise trip to San Diego yesterday." He took a long sip, then forked a clam, taking his time dipping it into the sauce.

"And she looked you up?" Pam prodded.

"Yep. She wanted to pick up where we left off."

"Then that's what you're going to do. That's why you're so happy!"

"You're getting ahead of me," he protested. "Don't you want to know why she changed her mind?"

"Of course," Pam said dutifully, realizing he wanted to savor it all to the fullest. "Why?"

"Because her career bombed, and now she's ready to get married and settle down." He hesitated, and this time she didn't try to rush him. "I waited for the thrill. I was finally getting what I'd always wanted, and I should have felt great. But I didn't, Pam." He took a deep breath. "I didn't feel anything—not hate, not love, not anything except a funny kind of surprise that I'd ever believed I wanted her."

"So it's over," she whispered.

"It's finally over, and I've never felt so free, so whole." He pushed the basket toward Pam. "You're not doing your share here."

While she helped herself to another plateful, he said sheepishly, "I want to thank you, Pam, for putting up with me all this time. I must have come across like a lovesick jerk." His smile twisted. "And for being so sweet about that desperate, insulting proposal." He picked up her hand. "But you knew it was an impulsive attempt to ease my pain and despair, not fair, as you said, to either one of us. Thanks for being so understanding, Pam. I do love you, but as a friend, not as a lover."

"I know," she said, "and I'm so glad you're free now, Alan. She didn't deserve you."

With a grateful squeeze, he let go of her hand. For the next few minutes her own heartache was blessedly buried underneath her happiness for Alan.

CHAPTER NINETEEN

Pam was trailing behind Alan in The Seahorse as he headed toward the cashier's desk when she came to a dead stop at the sound of a deep, familiar voice.

Turning sharply, she saw Cole in one of the booths, deep in earnest conversation as he leaned forward toward the exceptionally pretty girl across from him. Unseen herself behind their partially opened curtain, but unable to make out the words, Pam watched the pleading expression on Cole's face, the rapt way the girl was listening.

She moved on woodenly. By the time

Alan had paid the check, she'd swallowed her tears.

She kept them back all the way to their apartment building, even managing little listening sounds while Alan outlined all his new plans for playing the field.

But her thoughts were all on Cole, and she could actually feel the scalding bitterness knifing through her heartbreak. *He* wasn't having any trouble with a broken heart. He certainly hadn't wasted any time finding a new girl. Or had that girl been the one he'd wanted all along? Poor, beautiful Natalie perhaps? Had it only been guilt he'd felt for her, Pam, not love at all?

The prospect of being alone in her own apartment where she could let go kept her going.

When they finally got there, the sight of Kate pulling up right behind them was the last straw.

"Perfect timing," Kate chirped.

They all stood around for a few minutes chatting, Kate explaining that she'd been in the neighborhood, Alan telling her where he and Pam had been, Pam squirming, wishing they'd both go away.

Alan did. "I'll leave you girls to your gossip," he said good-naturedly as he headed toward his door.

Then Kate started up the steps, Pam following helplessly.

"I've never seen Alan so happy," Kate said as soon as they were inside and she'd plopped down on the sofa bed.

"I've got a pitcher of iced tea," Pam offered, glad at least they were going to talk about Alan. "I'll get it, and then I'll tell you what happened." She escaped around the counter into the tiny kitchen, resigning herself to another postponement.

After she'd told Kate all about Alan's good news, Kate exulted, "Sounds like all three of us have our love life in good shape now."

That was when Pam's overdue tears spilled out.

Kate was beside her in a second, her face suddenly puckered with anxiety. "Lovers' quarrel?" she asked softly.

"No lover," Pam blubbered, grinding

her fists into her eyes. "It's over. We were
right that day Mrs. Brooks gave it away.
Cole *was* the one who hit me."

"Oh, hon." Kate cradled her in her
arms. "When you didn't call me, I assumed everything was all right. And
you've been so cheerful ever since. I
didn't see any sense in bringing it up."

"It was an act," Pam confessed bitterly.
"I couldn't bear to go into it. I guess I
thought it would be easier after I was
finished working there."

"What did he say?" Kate gasped.

Pam shook her head helplessly. "He
admitted everything. Even giving me
the job to clear his conscience."

"Why didn't you walk out then and
there?" Kate asked.

"I did quit," Pam said dully, "but I
agreed to give him two weeks' notice.
And that was a week ago." Then she told
Kate about seeing Cole with that girl at
The Seahorse. "So everything was a lie,
even the part about being in love with
me."

"I don't see how you can go through
another week," Kate said.

"I can't," Pam agreed. "I never want to see him or that place again." She looked at Kate through a blur, and suddenly she was glad Kate was there. Somehow sharing it all did help!

Together they worked out the details.

"I'm sure I didn't leave any of my personal effects there," Pam said. "And the finished watercolors he wanted for the Los Angeles branch are all lined up on my shelf. If he really does want them," she added. "If it wasn't another piece of compensating busy work."

"It doesn't matter," Kate said. "You earned every penny you got there, and now we have to decide on the best way to let them know you're through."

In the end they agreed Pam should mail her resignation.

Sorry I'm unable to stay another week —Pamela Harper, she wrote, addressing the envelope to Cole.

"If I put it out for the postman to pick up tomorrow," she told Kate, "it'll get there Tuesday. Cole may or may not be in Los Angeles. Nobody knows his schedule these days. But if he isn't there,

Jerry might open it and relay the message."

Jerry! The new kind of grudging respect in his smile instead of the old look had been the only good thing about this last week. Not that it mattered anymore! He still thought the worst about her, and he'd probably be glad she was gone. Doubly glad if Cole rehired the Enright Agency!

"Someday we'll laugh about this, hon," Kate said when she left.

Pam gave her a grateful hug. "You said that before," she reminded her friend, "and we aren't laughing yet."

"We will," Kate predicted.

Pam went to bed that night too angry to cry anymore. If Cole could recover so quickly, so could she.

CHAPTER TWENTY

Pam woke groggily at the ring of the doorbell early the next morning. In her bare feet and robe, too befuddled to wonder who it was, her hair in total disarray, she flung the door open.

As she stared at the pretty face she'd seen with Cole yesterday afternoon, she came wide awake. When she shrank back from the unexpected confrontation, the girl walked in. Pam never did know how the door got closed.

"My name's Natalie Shearer." It was a shy, hesitant voice. "I was engaged to

Cole's brother."

So it was true. Pam had known it—feared it—all along. Cole loved Natalie.

Pam collapsed onto the end of the unmade sofa bed.

"Cole told me you know now it was his car that hit you that day," Natalie whispered, sinking down at the other end. "He said you thought he was driving." As she dissolved into tears, Pam stared at her blankly, wondering vaguely why she was here. "He said I had to clear it up," Natalie sobbed. "He said if I didn't go to the police and tell them I ran that light that day, he would." She mopped futilely at her eyes. "He won't go with me. And I—I'm afraid."

Too confused to absorb all the new meanings, Pam whispered, "Why the police?"

"He said you'd never believe him. He said it had to be *proved* to you."

Pam listened with growing dismay as the distraught girl sobbed out the pitiful story.

"I lived a life of quiet desperation before I met Norman. All I did was keep

house for my father. I didn't go anywhere. I never saw anyone. I was terri-
fied of everything and everybody. My
engagement to Norman was the first
time I ever defied my father." Her voice
choked away, then came back hoarsely. "I
was in love with Norm, but it was even
more than that. He gave me the promise
of a whole new life. When he died, everything else died—the love, the future, the
hope."

"But Cole wouldn't let you give up,"
Pam said.

Natalie shook her head. "Norm had
been secretly teaching me to drive," she
whimpered, "even though my father had
forbidden it. That day Cole was making
me keep at it. When he told me to put my
foot on the brake, I put it on the accelera-
tor by mistake, and we shot forward.
Cole grabbed the wheel. He yelled at me
to stop. But I couldn't. My father would
have killed me—will kill me when he
finds out." She shivered. "I told Cole I'd
never, ever drive again."

Natalie covered her face with her
hands, and Pam had to strain to hear the

rest of the tear-drenched words that oozed out. "But Cole loves you so much, he doesn't care what happens to me anymore."

Pam sidled over and folded the hysterical girl into her arms, her thoughts whirling dizzily as the words began to penetrate with new meaning. Cole wasn't in love with Natalie. He really was in love with her!

"You don't have to go to the police," Pam heard herself say. "I believe you. And your secret is safe with me."

Natalie's hands dropped. She stared at Pam through blurry eyes. "Do you mean you'll tell Cole you believe me?"

Pam nodded. "But will you do something for me?"

"Anything," Natalie promised fervently.

"Let Cole and me give you some more driving lessons."

Natalie's eyes widened in astonishment. "Even after—"

"Even after," Pam laughed. "It'll all work out. You'll see."

* * *

After Natalie left, Pam reveled in all the beautiful new information. How typical of Cole to protect Natalie all this time at his own expense. Of course he hadn't been drunk. The car had lurched because he'd tried to stop it.

And that was why he'd been out with Natalie yesterday—to tell Natalie she had to clear him. Because he loved *her!* Pam should have known he couldn't stop. Wasn't deep trust supposed to be vital to love? And she did love him so much. She vowed she'd never, ever doubt Cole again, no matter how things looked.

Suddenly remembering the awful note she'd written, she couldn't wait to shred it into a million pieces. Thank goodness she hadn't had a chance to mail it!

Her thoughts splintered. She and Kate had had it all wrong. She'd have to tell Kate how it really was. Kate would be so happy for her. But first she had to make it right with Cole.

Pam rushed to the phone, dialing his mother's number. He'd be there today. When she heard the gruff, "Bradshaw here," a sudden thread of panic skittered through her.

"This is Pam." Her voice came out thin and squeaky, but she kept pushing it. "I'm wondering if the beach is on my agenda today."

She heard Cole's gasp of surprise, then the carefully controlled eagerness in his voice. "Can I pick you up at one?"

"One will be fine." Her voice came out right this time.

Pam was bubbling with love and joy when Cole arrived.

"You've forgiven me," he said humbly. "Do I dare ask why?"

"I'll tell you all about it on the way."

"Now," he begged, sinking down on the sofa and pulling her down beside him.

Securely nestled in the circle of his arms, she told him all about Natalie's visit. "I believed her," she finished. "Will you forgive me for not trusting you?" It seemed so incredible now that she could have imagined this wonderful man capable of such a cowardly deed.

"If you'll believe me when I say I know how I was crazy to think the end result was all that mattered—to think I could devise a way to camouflage the truth." He gave Pam a chaste kiss on the forehead and added softly, "And if you'll believe me when I say I'll love you forever."

"If you'll believe me when I say it's the same with me," she bargained.

"What is?" he asked innocently.

She giggled. "I'll love you forever."

His arm tightened possessively. "I'm glad Nat didn't have to stir up her old man."

"I feel so sorry for her," Pam said. "I wish we could really help her."

"We will," Cole promised, his arm going slack as he fumbled in his pocket. Then he reached for Pam's left hand. "I've been carrying this around for these last two hideous weeks."

Her throat filled with awe as she stared at the sparkling diamond on her finger.

"Will you marry me, darling?"

"I'll be proud to," Pam quivered.

He kissed her again, but this time on her lips with such a searing passion, she tingled all the way to her toes.

Finally released, Pam tightened her arms around his neck and let her thoughts put it all together in a brand new, fulfilling way. Love was like a circle, almost as if it was meant to be, as if Fate had contrived it.

Why, if it hadn't been for the accident ... If she hadn't lost the Farnsworth's job ... If she hadn't discovered the awful truth and rebelled at Cole's deceit, forcing him to uncover the big lie and free them all ...

If Fate hadn't made all that happen, where would Pam be now?

"Let's go tell Mom she's going to have a daughter." All in one smooth motion, Cole picked her up as he stood.

"I love you," Pam whispered, savoring the beautiful words.